The Friendly Invasion – as the US GIs trained for D-Day

A drama-documentary – fact and fiction brought together

Alan Dearling

The Friendly Invasion – *as the US GIs trained for D-Day*

First published in 2011
Enabler Publications
45 Haymon's Cove
Eyemouth
Berwickshire
Scotland TD14 5EG
www.enablerpublications.co.uk

isbn: 978-0-9523316-8-1

Cover and text design by Oliver Carfrae and Alan Dearling

Printed on FSC stock from sustainable sources by: Hobbs the Printers, Totton.

The Friendly Invasion – as the US GIs trained for D-Day

A drama-documentary – fact and fiction brought together

Alan Dearling

Contents

Photo credits

With thanks for: front cover top and back cover top, p1, p9, p51 and p107, Alan Dearling's postcard/photo collection; p63, Alan Dearling; front cover bottom right, back cover bottom, title page, p17 and p71, US National Archives & Records Administration (public domain); p31, p41 and p97, Lyme Regis Philpot Museum; front cover bottom left, p85, p127, p161 and p171, Orchard Publications (public domain); p147, supplied by John Dover.

1.

Lyme Regis: late September 1943

The Cobb, Lyme Regis – before the war

It was nearly low tide as Jo looked across from the Cobb Gate towards the low-slung rocky outcrop jutting from the beach, and known locally as Lucy's Ledge. A further half a mile in the distance she had a clear view of the famous Cobb harbour. All along the shore, as far as she could see, were rolls of barbed wire and a number of ugly reinforced concrete anti-tank blocks. Jo was deep in thought as only a nearly-fifteen-year-old can be. *'Christ, I'm lonely. I wish I could be back in Plymouth. Sod the Germans. Sod the bombing...What a shithole this is now...closed up like a prison camp with concrete dragons' teeth on the beach, and sentries at either end of the Marine Parade promenade.'*

"Hi Jo!" a young airman on guard duty at the entrance to the parade called out.
"Do you want to slip along with your dog to Monmouth Beach? I'm sure I can 'not notice you', if you're quick through my gate. You know you really need a special pass."

"Thanks, Den, that's wonderful of you, the old mutt could do with a stretch of his legs. I hate not being able to go down to the beaches."
Jo and her mutt, who was actually a black and white mongrel called Prince belonging to her landlady, slipped by the sentry emplacement, with a backward, *"Thanks again."*

Following Prince's nose for new and old smells, Jo meandered an erratic path along the Marine Parade, with its olde worlde thatch cottages, and the imposing but odd, almost-folly-like, Sundial House. Prince took a fair few opportunities for pee stops at various railings along the way. At the end of the Parade Jo was confronted by a second checkpoint, again manned, this time by an airman who Jo knew slightly by sight, but not by name.
"Good morning, your colleague said it was alright for me to take my dog down to Monmouth Beach. Is that alright with you too?"
"I suppose so, but don't go right down to the beach and remember that the harbour is mined."
Jo gave the man her biggest smile, adding, *"My name's Jo, maybe see you at one of the dances."*
"Sure, but get lost now while I'm still looking the other way."

Jo was slightly taller than average, a somewhat gangly,

tomboy-style girl. Today, her brownish hair was tied back, but she looked a bit older than her age, with quite striking features which could turn a few male heads. But she took the hint and dragged Prince from snuffling round the sentry box and along the back of the closed-up Royal Standard pub. Beyond the Parade's end, Jo got a good view of the bustle of activity around two air-sea rescue launches in the ancient setting of the Cobb harbour. There was still a dreadful foreboding that Hitler's planned invasion might actually take place. It was quite common knowledge that it was codenamed Operation Sealion.[1] Lyme Regis was rumoured to be at the edge of the invasion plan, which would have seen German troops embarking from Cherbourg and making landfall between Charmouth and Seaton.

About a dozen men were busy moving heavy-looking boxes from a pill box structure on the Cobb down to the boats. Jo gave them a wave, which drew a couple of whistles from the men, as she went on towards a huge concrete slab of a place where all the local kids liked to hang out. It encased a big, round tunnel. From experience, Jo knew that if she could sneak in, it offered her and her dog a route down onto the beach. They made a quick dash through the tunnel and were able to drop down about three feet onto the stones at the other end. A man in uniform, obviously from the RAF barracks, was a little way down the beach with a companion. He

yelled, *"You be right careful, the harbour's mined and you shouldn't be on this beach."*
"I'll be careful, mister," Jo called out as she ran westwards with Prince along the pebbled beach, tucked deep underneath the ever-changing features of landslips along the Undercliff. Like most of her relatively new friends in Lyme, Jo was pretty certain that there were no mines in the harbour, since a couple of old guys were still allowed to go out fishing, but no matter.

Ten minutes later and Jo returned to the bottom of the Cobb Road and yet another sentry check-point. But this time, as she was obviously leaving the prohibited area, the man on duty just waved her through. She was then able to plod up the very steep, winding hill to Pound Road, across past the old Cottage Hospital to Silver Street, and thence down into Woodmead Road. Woodmead slopes steeply down towards the area of Lyme known as Jericho, the little trickle of the River Lim and the Laundry. It was there in a house called 'Lavenders', half-way down on the left-hand side of Woodmead Road, that Jo and her friend from Plymouth were billeted with Mr and Mrs Green, whose home had been a guest house until the outbreak of the war. Now they made some extra money from offering half a dozen evacuees a meagre 'home from home'. In return, the government paid the Greens twelve shillings and sixpence for temporarily housing each child who was still at school.

Jo dried off some of the mud from Prince's feet on a towel left for the purpose inside the porch and called out, *"I'm home,"* to no-one in particular. Prince lollopped with his tongue hanging out towards his water bowl in the back kitchen. Jo went up to the first floor, to the room at the back of the house which she and her friend Ruth shared. Ruth was a dark-haired, petite Jewish girl. Her family were from Poland, but she and her mother had left in the mid-1930s and had moved to England. At first they had lived with relatives in London, but had settled in Plymouth just before the outbreak of war.

It was time for the girls to get ready for the Grammar School where she and Ruth would meet some of their old friends from Dame Alleyn's School in Plymouth and some new friends they'd made in Lyme. *'At least the Lyme Grammar School is mixed,'* she thought, in a rather more positive frame of mind then when she had set off on her walk down to the Cobb.
"Come on sleepyhead," Jo yelled at Ruth, pulling off her friend's bedcover, *"schooltime."*

2.

Services of Supply: early October 1943

Pre-war Broad Street

Much of the area and paths around the Undercliff were heavily mined, since Lyme had been anticipated as a potential target for Hitler's invasion forces. This made 'playing' for the local kids in the area more than a mite dangerous. So, ginger-haired Ricky, who had been evacuated from Surrey, was currently confined to base. He was enjoying daydreaming, sitting on the swing in the front garden of his grandparent's bungalow. His thoughts were far away from the Devon and Dorset border. In particular he was thinking of his Scottish father, Terry, who had been recently promoted to the rank of Major in the British Eighth Army, following the North African campaign under the command of Bernard Montgomery. At the moment, Ricky wasn't even sure where his father was.

The bungalow, near Pinhay House, sat just off the edge of the main coast road from Lyme Regis to Seaton. A distant rumble attracted Ricky's attention. It sounded like nothing he'd ever heard in his thirteen years. The noise was getting louder and even more formidable. It

was coming closer from the direction of Seaton. Ricky rushed into his grandparents' home, yelling:
"Come look, Come look...it's something enormous... come on grandma, grandpa."

The Stevens came out and were as startled as their grandson.
"What in damnation is it?" cried out Grandpa Stevens. Then, like the legendary 7th Cavalry, the apparition of huge army trucks started to pour, one after another, past the house in the direction of Lyme.
"Yeeehaw!!!" yelled one giant of a black Corporal (but referred to in Britain, as coloured) from the front of an American jeep. More unfamiliar American voices, except from the movies, cheered and whooped as they spotted their English audience.
"Here comes the cavalry!"
"Ike's boys are here to save you!"
Ricky was suddenly aware of a shower of missiles sailing over his head. They landed around him and his grandparents, scattered across the grass verge below the hedge outside his grandparents'. The noise of the convoy roared on towards Lyme as Ricky scavenged the 'missiles' up together. They turned out to be an array of wrapped sugar cubes, chewing gum, Chelsea candy and Hershey bars. A veritable treasure trove of sweets – perhaps more than a month's ration.

It really was a scene from the silver screen. Afterwards, Ricky told his school friends, perhaps just exaggerating a tiniest, wee bit in true Scottish fashion: *"There must have been two, three hundred of 'em...them Americans, the Yanks...and all a hollering, 'n a shouting. Youse should've been there."* Ricky's friends at the Grammar School saw Ricky as something of a leader. He'd been one of the first evacuees to arrive in the town and perhaps because he was billeted with his grandparents had quickly settled in. Unlike some of his fellow evacuees, Ricky as an 'incomer' seemed more 'exotic' and worldly-wise than most of them. In fact, he had an older head on his young shoulders.

In reality, no-one counted the trucks, jeeps and wagons or the stranger looking vehicles with tank-type tracks that rumbled along the tarmac road. They drove down the steep descent, past the decidedly odd, circular, thatched, Umbrella Cottage, and on into a sleepy and unsuspecting Lyme Regis, noisily making their arrival obvious even to the most elderly and hard-of-hearing local residents. And there were more than a few of them in the autumn of 1943, with nearly all the able-bodied, fit for service or war work, men and women drafted away.

The convoy of American GIs were in fact the 'advance troops', ordered into the area by the ETO, the European

Theater of Operations. These were the Services of Supply (SOS) and Engineer Special Brigade (ESB) troops. They were the US army's builders, engineers, drivers and cooks. Their jobs were to build camps, erect tents and Quonset huts, dig trenches, set up the mess areas and help to requisition the billets, buildings and special facilities needed for the combat troops who were to arrive in the area after them.

The noise-full cavalcade of mostly black faces, still cheering and caterwauling, swept on like a human avalanche, from Sidmouth Road into Pound Street and thence into Lyme's main thoroughfare, Broad Street. By this point, the oncoming racket, the smells and mayhem generated by the troops, had brought out the locals onto the pavements on either side of the narrow main street. At the 'top of town', looking up Broad Street, outside of the old Volunteer Arms on the left-hand side and Watson's Garage on the right, shop girls, old men, mums with prams and a few workers exempt from the services' war effort, gazed, open-mouthed at the spectacle of grinning, yelling black faces. Or, as many remarked afterwards, black faces filled with such white teeth. The sight of the incoming army of occupation was awesome, but what lingered were the intriguing, unfamiliar smells. Grease, oil, fumes, the sweat of the military bodies – all accompanied by a cloying staleness. More candy bars were thrown from

the convoy as the Yanks kept up their 'conversations' with the totally baffled and bemused onlookers:
"Hiya, cutie, you OK for a walk out with me later?"
"Jeez, you've sure got a purty little village here."

The lead jeep led the rest of the troops down into the even narrower stretch of Bridge Street at the bottom end of town. Over the little bridge over the Buddle the troops flowed, startling a fair few ducks in the process. They then proceeded up Church Street. The convoy stopped abruptly just opposite the gruesome spikes of St Michael's Church, where local legend has it that James II's 'Hanging' Judge Jeffreys had impaled the heads of the twelve 'martyrs' who had supported Monmouth in the rebellion of 1685. The troops then turned sharp left into the single track confines of Poole's Court. From there they continued along past the Gas and Range Works and onto the track that was Corporation Terrace. They'd arrived at their personal destination. *"Wagons halt,"* ordered a white officer, getting into the spirit of the day.

America's mostly black advance troops had landed at the area known to locals as Laundry Flats, Mill Green. This was the 'friendly invasion' indeed.

Later that day many of the men were given leave to stop unloading the trucks and erecting the hundreds of bell tents. A group of them stripped to their waists and stood in the river bed washing off the grime and dust of the day. The men were horse-playing in the stream, their moistened dark chests reflecting the weak, last rays of the afternoon sun. A little girl stood beside her mother directly opposite the men, down the bank on the other side of the little River Lim. She hadn't immediately noticed the troops. *"Mummy, mummy, I don't like them,"* she exclaimed, immediately bursting into a torrent of tears. Like everyone in sleepy Lyme Regis she had never before seen hundreds of men all congregated together and certainly none with such dark skins.

3.

The tan Americans: October 1943

A battalion picnic for a visiting dignitary

"...here we have a very thickly populated country that is devoid of racial consciousness. They know nothing about the conventions and habits of polite society that have been developed in the U.S. in order to preserve a segregation in social activity without making the matter one of official or public notice. To most English people, including village girls – even those of perfectly fine character – the negro soldier is just another man, rather fascinating because he is unique in their experience, a jolly good fellow and with money to spend. Our own white soldiers, seeing a girl walk down the street with a negro, frequently see themselves as protectors of the weaker sex and believe it necessary to intervene even to the extent of using force, to let her know what she's doing."

Dwight D. Eisenhower, in a memo to General Surles in Washington, September 10th 1942. Ike was, by then, Commanding General, European Theater of Operations, based in London.

Doris Green was a good church-going Christian. At 'Lavenders', she and her husband Donald were discussing the Americans over supper with their seven paying guests. Doris remarked, *"Well they are here and they seem very polite."*
Donald responded, *"...but you know what Mrs May, the vicar's wife said..."*
"Well that was Mrs May, and that was Somerset. We're in Lyme in Dorset, and I think we should welcome our coloured guests," Doris quickly retorted.

"Do you remember what Mrs May recommended? It got reported in the 'Sunday Pictorial'. Umm. I think I put the article in the drawer. I'll just get it." After a little rummaging around, Donald returned and read aloud:
"Here's the six points she suggested that the English should adopt in relations with coloured Americans:
1. If a local woman keeps a shop and a coloured soldier enters, she must serve him, but she must do it as quickly as possible and indicate as quickly as possible that she does not desire him to come there again.
2. If she is in a cinema and notices a coloured soldier next to her, she moves to another seat immediately.
3. If she is walking on the pavement and a coloured soldier is coming towards her, she crosses to the other pavement.

4. If she is in a shop and a coloured soldier enters, she leaves as soon as she has made her purchase or before that, if she is in a queue.
5. White women, of course, must have no social relationship with coloured troops.
6. On no account must coloured troops be invited to the homes of white women." [2]

"That's awful," blurted out Jo.
"I'm a bit frightened of them," said Ruth, *"also, I've been brought up not to mix with non-Jews and, err, schwartzes...sorry, I shouldn't have said that. That's rude. And, I've really really learned a lot being here with you. But, it's that my family are quite strict. It's all so strange."*
Jo responded, *"I remember when you had to eat with us all the first time. It was obviously difficult for you. But then, I have no idea about how Jews live. You're the first Jewish person I've ever actually met."*
Doris Green chipped in, *"Well my dear, this war is responsible for a lot. And now we've got all these American troops here getting ready for the second front. I'm sure they're feeling lonely and 'strange' here too."*
Jo couldn't resist saying, *"They keep on giving me what they call candy and gum, and they seem, err, well, nice, I guess."*
Another of the evacuees, James, joined in saying,

"Our headmaster, Mr Freeman at the Grammar, told us the eleventh commandment is: 'Don't ask for gum, chum'."

Doris, who was looking thoughtful, added, *"Well the ladies at our church have had a long discussion and agreed that we're going to make the American boys feel welcome. The ladies have heard that the coloured ones are good singers and are very religious back where they come from...and so, that's decided then...what I think we should do as a family. I'm going to get in touch with their commanding officer and invite some of the boys round to tea on Sunday."*

"Well, I don't know..." muttered Donald.
"That's settled then," replied Doris.

The next morning, Doris got out her best writing pad and wrote a note which she placed in an envelope. She'd addressed it to the 'Commander of the American GIs, Laundry Fields, Lyme Regis'. A little later she put on her coat and scarf and informed Donald that she was off into town to collect the rations and to deliver her note to the Americans. On her return a couple of hours later, a flushed Doris Green reported that she'd actually been invited in to meet a captain and he'd readily agreed to send up four of 'his boys' the next Sunday at four o'clock for tea. Doris added, *"The camp is amazing. Hundreds of tents; a big mess tent with the coloured troops waiting on the officers. Everywhere, lots of activity, and I heard that the troops are busy up the Spittles building another camp on the hill below the golf course, and the same again besides the Sidmouth Road above Ware Cliffs. I saw them bringing pebbles off the beach to construct trackways between the tents and a main track up to Cloverdale Garage on the Charmouth road. The captain also thanked me and the other ladies at St Michael and St George's for setting up the rest room for the troops with the gramophone player and the Tommy Dorsey, Glenn Miller and Bing Crosby records."*

Everyone at the 'Lavenders' had been preening themselves and the kitchen had been a hive of activity. The best china had appeared from the cabinet and the ration books had taken a hard hit. The knock on the door was army-punctual, exactly on 4 p.m. Doris and Donald opened the door together. Outside, four very nervous young black GIs stood in their olive green denims, replete with big, slightly lopsided grins.
"Mr and Mrs Green? Corporal Jarvis and Privates Harden, Dempsey and Marvin."
Doris couldn't help thinking that none of them looked any older than her own two sons who were stationed up north. Her heart went out to them, especially considering how the 'Mrs Mays' of the world were

trying to make them feel rejected.

"Well, you come on in and meet our family," Donald replied shaking the corporal's hand, and adding, *"I'm Donald Green and this is my wife, Doris. We have seven guests staying with us, all evacuees from Plymouth. You've perhaps heard that city has been badly bombed."* Doris led the way for the GIs, *"We thought you could take tea with us and we've prepared sandwiches and cakes in the main lounge, as we don't have enough room at the dining table."*

Jo, Ruth and the others were already sitting in the lounge as the Greens brought in their American guests. Another round of introductions was made. Corporal Jarvis took the lead on behalf of the four GIs and gradually as the group chatted, everyone began to relax a bit, as tea was poured and plates and sandwiches were handed around. Though, in truth, balancing plates on laps wasn't the easiest of exercises.

The corporal produced some cigarettes, Lucky Strikes, and a selection of Babe Ruth and Hershey bars as gifts for the family to share out, saying, *"We've set up a PX store where our troops can buy plenty of things and we'll be using your Marine Theatre as our main recreation area and what you'd call the NAAFI."*

For much of the soldiers' visit the evacuees were unusually quiet. In fact they were very much in awe of their guests, sneaking sidelong looks at the dark men in impressive uniforms. But the Greens did their best to get the GIs to feel at home. They asked the soldiers how they had travelled down to Lyme, and the corporal, whose first name was Eugene, explained that he and his colleagues had come from Manhattan on the RMS Queen Mary, which had docked into Liverpool. He said, *"Us coloured boys, we had to bunk down on four-tiered 'shelves' right down in the bottom of the ship. We was tossed and churned every which way."* Eugene then described the next phase of their journey where they had been herded into special trains with blackouts and brought down at first to a camp on Salisbury Plain.
"Jeez, it was just like being on a never-ending subway train." Then Eugene added, *"And our subways back home where Franklin here and myself live in Dallas, are good n' open, not like the little boxes we rode in on the way here."*
Donald, keen to change the conversation on to a more positive note, said, *"Well, at least you're here in one spot for a while now. Plenty of good Dorset fresh air an' all."*

Jo had been dying to ask the soldiers a question and finally plucked up the courage, *"I've always wondered what GI stands for?"*

Eugene's Dallas compatriot, Franklin, answered, *"I didn't know for certain either. I kind of thought it meant 'government issue' for a long while, but I been told it actually means 'galvanised iron' which is pretty strange."*
"You hardly look old enough to be over here," Doris interjected.
Eugene quickly replied on Franklin's behalf, *"Well maam, he's our 'baby'. I know his older brother back in Dallas. Franklin's just 18. I promised to keep an eye on him, keep him OK over here in your country. Actually, none of us are that old. Just feels like we're growing up real fast, and a long way from home and familiar things we know."*

After about an hour, the Greens tidied up the tea things and got the evacuees to show the GIs round the garden, which had mostly been cultivated for growing vegetables and fruit as part of the 'Dig for Victory' war effort which everyone was encouraged to do. They were also shown the metal Anderson air-raid shelter which the Greens had had installed at the bottom of the garden. Just before 6 p.m. the men said it was time for them to go back to their camp, and Eugene thanked the Greens for their *"very fine chow,"* which raised a laugh. He added that he hoped that they would have the pleasure of inviting the family to one of the entertainments, courtesy of the US army, *"once the rest of the troops arrived"*. This news came as a bit of shock, as no-one was really meant to know what the Americans were doing in Dorset and Devon, but of course, gossip about the planned invasion and liberation of France was rife.

Just before leaving, Eugene again thanked the Greens and said,
"You've been real swell to us. It means a lot to us boys. A story I heard perhaps tells you a truth that we're living a testament to. Just up your neighbouring county, a rich lady did the same as you. Contacted the commanding officer and asked him to send round six of his troops for tea. But she said specifically; make sure there's no Jews. Sunday came around and the six troops arrived at the lady's door. Six troops just like us, coloured boys from the Southern states. Well, the lady was aghast and says, 'Surely there's been a mistake?' So, our boy replies, right quickly, 'No maam, Colonel Cohen never makes mistakes'."

Franklin couldn't help himself and quickly added, *"I miss back home, but we still got the segregation in Dallas. And the Klansman, the members of the Ku Klux Klan, they still purty strong in our city. Back in the 1920s they had more than 13,000 members including the mayor, the sheriff, and most of the police and lawyers. They even burned 'KKK' in acid in one coloured boy's forehead, jus' for speaking to a white lady in an elevator."*

Like Franklin, Ruth blurted out, *"Me and my parents were all born in Lodz in Poland. And before we left, the Nazis had begun ransacking and burning our shops and homes. My mutti, my mother I mean, and myself, we escaped before it got too bad. But after we left, the Germans began interning members of our communities, our rabbis even, for making a stand. They were building a ghetto for the Jews...We then heard that my father had been killed. We landed up in Plymouth, but then came the bombing, so here I am. Luckily, I could already speak English."*

The others in the room looked at her in a shocked silence. She hadn't spoken much to the other evacuees about her family and background – perhaps trying to 'fit in' more by ignoring her Jewishness – and simply trying to behave as just another girl who was from Plymouth.

"We have a lot in common, maam," Eugene commented, *"we know 'bout people hating us."* A few tears had started to trickle from the corner of Ruth's eyes. Taking out a clean handkerchief from one of his top jacket pockets, Eugene handed it to Ruth, *"Here*

missee, don't you be letting yourself get so sorrowful."

Eugene took the silence that followed as his cue to muster his men, and with a further round of goodbyes, the Americans took their leave. Once they'd left, Doris said, *"Well, I think we did our duty."* After helping clear up the tea things, the evacuees decamped to their rooms. Back in their bedroom, Jo confided with Ruth, *"Eugene and Franklin seem like good blokes. They all do. I think it's time us schoolgirls start to turn ourselves into young women. It's too good an opportunity!"*

Ruth was a bit shell-shocked by the whole encounter. She was feeling particularly alien. Alone and lonely. She thought about the coloured Americans. She took a moment to consider her own situation, then said, *"It's alright for you, Jo. I'm Jewish. We don't...we aren't supposed to think about boys, men. You know what I mean."*

4.

Little America: around Christmas time 1943

A girl in a US military vehicle in Lyme

"British money is in pounds, shillings and pence. They won't be pleased to hear you call it 'funny money'. They sweat hard to get it... [and] won't think any better of you for throwing money around. The British 'Tommy' is apt to be specially touchy about the difference between his wages and yours."

From 'Instructions for American Servicemen in Britain', published in 1942 and given to all the visiting soldiers.

The 1st battalion of the American 16th Infantry regiment arrived into Lyme Regis in early November 1943 direct from active duty in Tunisia and Sicily as part of Operation Torch. These were the combat troops, the fighting troops, unlike the Services of Supply GIs who had arrived earlier. Their regiment was part of the US 1st Infantry Division, known popularly as the 'Big Red One', which was soon spread liberally around the district. Approximately ninety per cent of the 1st Division were white GIs; many from the southern states of America. The local battalion Commanding Officer, Captain Charles M. Hangsterfer, known as 'Hank', plus his immediate staff lived at The Chalet in Langmoor Gardens, an imposing colonial-style building, whilst company officers were billeted at the Hotel Alexandra. Many of the infantry men lived in tented camps on Ware Cliffs, Spittles and a few down in the Laundry Fields with the Services of Supply troops. To fit them in, a few Nissen-type huts, called Quonsets, were erected. Virtually every hotel and spare room in the town was requisitioned as a billet for soldiers. The main 1st batallion HQ was located in the old school premises used by A. S. Neill's famous Summerhill School from 1923-27.[3] The local 'C' Company headquarters was established in a big house, Woodville, in Silver Street and their HQ staff were quartered in the Old Monmouth Hotel in Church Street.

With the new wave of troops came an amazing selection of US army equipment and vehicles. There were amphibious trucks, giant transporters laden with tanks, half-track scout cars and even bulldozers – totally unknown in Britain. GIs trooped throughout the town, often marching and chanting in their sing-song, call and response style known by them as 'Jodies'.[4] Children were especially captivated by the Americans and were the eager recipients of 'treats', ranging from candy bars and chewing gum to short trips in military vehicles. Careering military vehicles of all shapes and sizes became common everywhere. Much to the amusement of the locals, one truck got wedged between a house and a garden wall whilst trying to navigate down the ever-narrowing Sherborne Lane. The GIs even practised using flamethrowers in the Hatchett fields behind Woodmead Road. This generated much muttering in the hedgerows and over the picket fences around the town. Lyme lived in something of a bubble of its own making and didn't take too kindly to incomers at the best of times. Now, with most of the local men enlisted or conscripted, those who were left were particularly set in their ways. But that was changing rapidly as the war had suddenly come to Lyme. Having some singed foliage and a few startled cows was a minor aggravation in the bigger scheme of things.

Finding their way around Lyme, with its narrow lanes, footpaths, short-cuts, back passages and the maze of ups and downs, was proving a daily puzzle for the Americans. Indeed, many of them spent much of their time asking directions. After a few weeks in the town, one of the GIs, who was a bit of an amateur map-maker, had produced his own little map of Lyme and its environs, showing the camps and other key locations. This was much copied by the rest of the regiment.

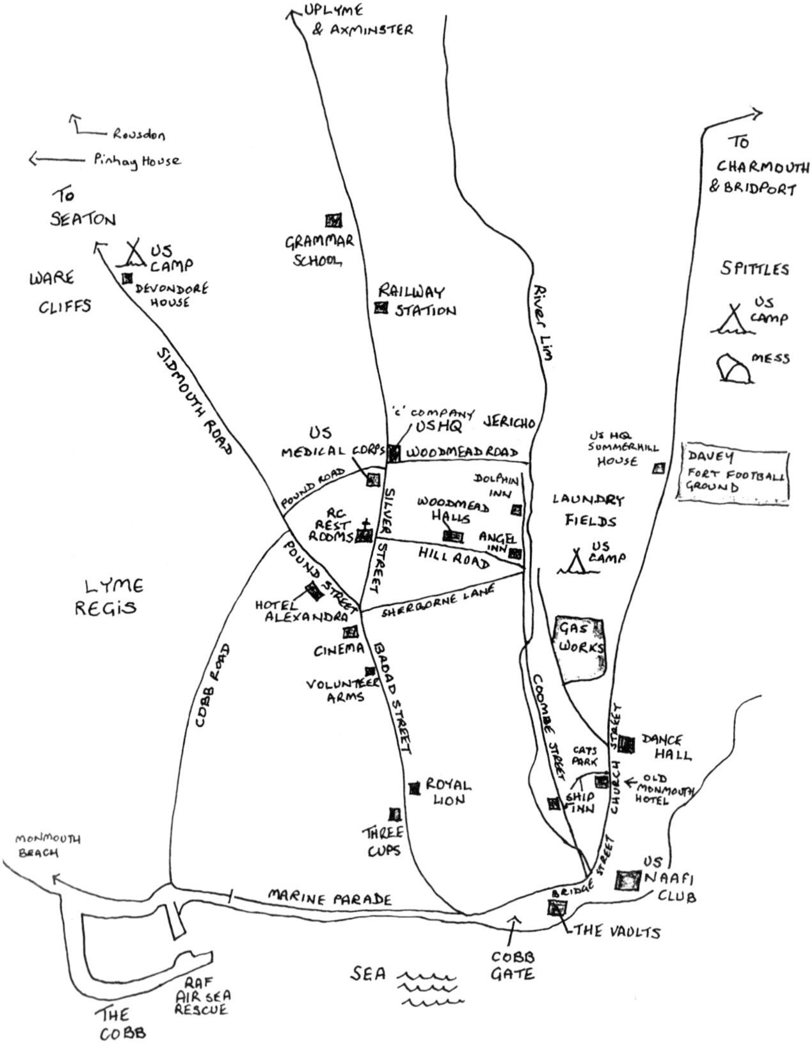
UPLYME
& AXMINSTER
Rousdon
Pinhay House
TO
SEATON
US
CAMP
WARE
CLIFFS
DEVONDORE
HOUSE
GRAMMAR
SCHOOL
RAILWAY
STATION
River Lim
TO
CHARMOUTH
& BRIDPORT
SPITTLES
US
CAMP
MESS
SIDMOUTH ROAD
'C' COMPANY
USHQ
JERICHO
US
MEDICAL CORPS
WOODMEAD ROAD
US HQ
SUMMERHILL
HOUSE
DAVEY
FORT FOOTBALL
GROUND
POUND ROAD
DOLPHIN
INN
WOODMEAD
HALLS
LAUNDRY
FIELDS
RC
REST
ROOMS
SILVER STREET
ANGEL
INN
US
CAMP
HILL ROAD
POUND STREET
LYME
REGIS
HOTEL
ALEXANDRA
SHERBORNE LANE
GAS
WORKS
CINEMA
BROAD STREET
COBB ROAD
VOLUNTEER
ARMS
COOMBE STREET
CHURCH STREET
DANCE
HALL
CARS
PARK
OLD
MONMOUTH
HOTEL
ROYAL
LION
SHIP
INN
THREE
CUPS
MONMOUTH
BEACH
US
NAAFI
CLUB
BRIDGE STREET
MARINE PARADE
THE VAULTS
COBB
GATE
SEA
RAF
AIR SEA
RESCUE
THE
COBB

Sitting in the Dolphin Inn, old Lyme locals, Jim Howden and Jack Wedlock reflected on the changes that the troops' arrival had brought to the town. Down at the millstream on the edge of Lyme's old town, the Dolphin was a very traditional old 'local' pub, offering farm ciders, locally-sourced ales and also rooms for travellers.

"It's an American town now," muttered Jim supping ale from one of landlady Bowditch's tankards.
"You're right there, Jim. There must be over a thousand of 'em round about here. You knows I work at cinema and we gets more dollars there now than pounds, shillings and pence. They're great movie-goers, and on their wages they can afford to go whenever they fancy," Jack replied, lighting another American, Camel cigarette.
"But a lot of them do brag and show off. When I told one white GI the old one about them being 'Overpaid, over-sexed and over here', he snapped straight back that the Brits are 'Underpaid, under-sexed and under Eisenhower'."

From the next table bespectacled Ivy joined in the conversation, *"I've been working at their NAAFI in the Marine Theatre and all I can say is that we find the coloured fellas are much nicer to deal with...they're real courteous with a natural charm...me, I'd rather serve a regiment of dusky lads than a couple of the white troops we've got now."* Ivy's companion, Edith, chipped in, *"I work alongside Ivy and I've been walking out with one of the coloureds, Eugene. He's only 20, but he's a right gentleman. A real charmer, calls me 'his Duchess'. But when we came out from the cinema last week, a group of white GIs came over, and a big Southern States' sergeant yelled at Eugene, 'What are you black bastard doing on the sidewalk?' Then he took a swing at Eugene, knocked him down and another booted him in the ribs. Eugene shouted at him, 'Hey Sarge, I'm an American', and the sergeant yelled back, 'You're a chickenshit nigger; you'll always be a nigger.' Luckily, some of our local chaps came to rescue and the white GIs backed off. Afterwards, Eugene said to me he just couldn't win. He told me, 'If I'd've stumbled on a brick, they'd've said I was drunk n' beat me up for that'...I fear there's going to be real trouble sometime."*

"It's true," agreed Jack. *"We'd been told to segregate the cinema. We refused. But it seems the Americans have sorted it out internally between themselves. The white troops Tuesdays, Thursdays and Saturdays and the coloured ones on Wednesdays and Fridays. The snowdrops – the American Military Police – have been round all the pubs and hotels and designated ones like the Three Cups for officers only, and others like here*

are used just by the coloureds, and others like the Vaults and the Angel are only for the whites."
Jim replied, *"Well I heard Mr Churchill originally asked Roosevelt not to send any coloured troops here, but Roosevelt said that we had to have ten per cent coloureds, or none at all.*[5] *Then, a military bloke, Dowler I think his name was, came up with a set of notes. I was shown them by Jack down at the gasworks, as they are looking after a lot of the vehicles for the GIs and some for our army guys. I remember the gist of what it said. Along the lines that the coloured troops presents a new problem to us British men and women. That while they are American citizens, there is racial problem that cannot be ignored.*

Dowler wants us to change our attitudes so that it conforms to that of the white American citizen – in other words discrimination and segregation. In fact, he said that that the coloureds have 'a simple mental outlook' and that whites should avoid associating with them. Pretty damning stuff." [6]

"But that's not our British way," Edith added, *"I'm having none of it."*
Jim nodded his agreement, *"If they are good enough to come over here and fight for us...risk dying...they are as good as the next man, and better than many."*

5.

Free trade 1943-44

An un-named GI on guard in Lyme

Ricky had given up his paper-round. He'd never much liked cycling his tradesman's bike all the way from Pinhay, past Ware, and on down to the railway station just after six in the morning to collect the papers from the WH Smith's kiosk. Now, he'd found something altogether more lucrative. In fact, even though he was now just fourteen, he was making more money than most adults in Lyme. He hit on the idea when a group of the American soldiers living in the camp up by the old Devondore House had begun to ask him to collect things for them in town and bring them back to their camp. He remembered the first time he'd talked to the GIs, back in October.

"Hi there, buddy," the white GI just by the sentry gate to the camp had called out to him, *"you lookin' to make yourself some money?"*

"Well, for sure mister," Ricky had swiftly responded.

"See, I'm one the cooks. Name's Friedrich, but they all just call me Fred. Could you get me..." At this point, Fred's sergeant entered noisily into their conversation, roughly and rudely addressing Ricky: *"Quit the crap.*

You boy, you got any sisters?"
Ricky was a bit taken aback by this loud and arrogant man, but the sergeant wasn't one to be ignored. Ricky answered, *"Mister, I'm afraid I ain't got no sisters."*
"What about girl cousins?"
"None of them either."
The sergeant then made it patently clear what he wanted, saying, *"OK, well me, I got this itch. And this itch, I mean to get it well scratched. Know what I mean, boy? I been in action, plenty of medals. It's been kill or be killed, and I'm the one that's done the killing so far. But the next one may be my last, and Sergeant Henry knows what he wants. What about the Land Girls you got up at the farm?"*
Ricky replied, *"You know, I think they've all got themselves boyfriends with the RAF men down at the air-sea rescue place on the Cobb."* At this, the sergeant angrily took his leave, still muttering loudly about 'his needs'.

"Right, before we get interrupted again. Apologies for Sergeant Henry. He's a good soldier. The best when in battle. But..." Private Fred then changed his tone of voice and addressed Ricky quietly, *"Can you get me fresh produce? I cook in the kitchen for the officers down at the Three Cups Hotel."* Ricky considered this, and said he'd find out what he could lay his hands on.

Ricky's grandparents' bungalow was just on the edge of the Pinhay House estate, and Grandpa Stevens still worked part-time as an odd-jobbing gardener. Quite often Ricky helped him after school, and initially Ricky used his grandfather as the go-between with the farmer's wife, buying surplus eggs and fresh produce such as milk and cheese, and sometimes rabbits, which were plentiful in the areas not mined in the Undercliff.

Most days after school Ricky would call in to the door at the back of the Three Cups and collect orders from Fred the Chef. He had put two cloth panniers onto the front of his tradesman's bike and acquired an army haversack from Fred. When the farm couldn't produce enough eggs, Ricky had worked out an exchange scheme whereby he swapped 'balancer rations' of corn and poultry food with other farms in exchange for eggs. On his way into school he dropped eggs and other goods off at the Ware camp and they organised delivery to Fred. Ricky often witnessed the Ware camp virtually besieged by girls and women waiting none-too patiently outside the camp perimeters and guard points. Similar scenes were repeated at the camps in Laundry Fields and up on the landslip area called the Spittles. As in other areas of the south-west of England at the time, these young women became known as the 'camp followers', 'Yank-bashers', or sometimes 'spam-lovers', after the popular American canned meat.

Gradually, Ricky used his youthful charm with the wife of the farmer, Mrs Gale, in order to buy supplies and develop his business. This was supplemented by two additional sources. The first was the Land Girls. Ricky had already become besotted by young Grace, and was awkward and somewhat tongue-tied when in her company. She was about 17 and worked mostly in the dairy. On hot days, to the dismay and disapproval of Mrs Gale, Grace was to be seen wearing shorts and a home-made bra made from plaited scarves. Grace smoked and was partial to pairs of nylons. So, Ricky bought cartons of Lucky Strikes and nylons, plus cans of pineapple obtained through Fred the Chef, who could buy them at the US army PX store for about one-tenth of the English price, if indeed they could be obtained at any price. Ricky then traded these with Grace for further supplies of cream, cheese and other heavily rationed foods.

Filippo and Alphonso were another source of additional supplies for Ricky. They were two of the four Italian POWs who were dropped off at the farm six days a week from the prisoner of war camp on the outskirts of Axminster. They first worked on the potato harvest, then helped to tidy up the neglected orchard. As with Grace, Ricky was able to exchange cigarettes for fresh produce. Both the Italians had very dark complexions and spent a good deal of time on their hair and even

wore some make-up, which led to them being referred to as the 'Nancy Boys' by most of the male farm-hands. The Land Girls, however, thought they were incredibly handsome and loved their Italian language, especially when the Italian men called out to them:
"Ciao bella...cara...io te adoro."
Somehow, even Italian phrases like *"...molto molto fredo,"* meaning very, very cold, sounded exotic and ultra-romantic to the Land Girls.

In fact it was common gossip around the farms that some of the Land Girls had even managed to visit the Italians in Axminster. The POW camp was actually incredibly lax and quite a few of the 'residents' were occasionally able to obtain passes out in the evenings. The joke that was 'doing the rounds' was that the Italian men were even supplying cosmetics to the girls. Another success for international trade!

Ricky was destined for a further encounter with Sergeant Henry. The sergeant was completely unlike Fred the Chef, who had become something of a friend and older-brother figure in Ricky's life. Ricky was cycling in towards Lyme from Pinhay and spotted the sergeant standing with his hands in pockets, cigarette perched arrogantly in his lips. He was outside the high wall which surrounded Devondore House, which the American's had requisitioned. The sergeant, as a

platoon commander, had made himself more than at home. *"Over here, boy,"* the sergeant commanded, as Ricky got off his bicycle, which he had been riding back from school.
"It's time for some proper education for you," Henry said grabbing Ricky by the shoulders and pushing him in through the main door to Devondore. Henry locked the door behind him.
"I got some real adult entertainment laid on for you inside here," Henry uttered loudly as he pushed Ricky up the stairs and into a bedroom. There, lying on a double bed was Esme, whom Ricky recognised as the dark-eyed, small, slim Gypsy girl from the local village of Rousdon. She had briefly been in the class in the year above his, but rarely attended school.
"This is my squaw," Henry informed Ricky. *"She looks after the needs of me and my friends."* And added, *"She's a good learner, and she knows what's good for her and her father."*

Ricky later told his school friends a little of what happened next, remembering that the sergeant had afterwards given him a whole carton of 200 Lucky Strikes for his grandparents. Ricky recounted events, *"Sergeant Henry had two other pals with him…they went through strangest sexual performance you could possibly imagine with the girl…kept on calling her the 'squaw', with the sergeant trying to get me to go over and join them. I just couldn't, but when I got home to my grandparents, far later than usual, I rushed to my room. I didn't want them to see my trousers being all wet and sticky. My grandfather was well pleased with the 200 Lucky Strikes so didn't notice. I suspect he would also have enjoyed the afternoon's entertainment...I gather that Esme's father called in at the camp a couple of times each week and was given money and red petrol by the sergeant. Very soon he was able to replace his dilapidated old scrap van with a much newer lorry. Presumably, Esme was bringing home much much more than by selling a few pegs and firewood from house to house."*

After a pause, Ricky continued, *"You know, actually, I've left something out of my story. The next time I saw Sergeant Henry he tried to drag me back into Devondore, saying that he was going to lock me in the bunkroom with the squaw, whom he called his whore, and then bring his platoon along to watch me perform!...I didn't think he was joking, so I scarpered right quickly."*

By spring 1944, with the Americans outnumbering Lyme locals, Ricky had actually managed to establish his personal horticultural enterprise. It was complete with his own vegetable plot, cloches and he had managed to obtain the use of an old, redundant greenhouse. He grew and sold lettuces, early strawberries and more. Quite some enterprise for a boy of his age. But then, he'd used his wits to get on.

6.

Girl talk/Boy talk

Royal Lion Hotel, Broad Street

Ruth confided with Jo,*"I've been talking to Penny about joining the Land Army."* They were in their shared room at 'Lavenders' and had come upstairs after tea with the Greens and the other evacuees. Ruth added, *"My mother would be mortified. She expects me to work in an office, at worst, a factory. Our people, my family, don't work with our hands on the land. But since coming here, I find it attractive...my life is changing so fast, it's so different...and being among non-Jews. I'm beginning to hope I don't have to go back to living in a city."*

"I'm interested too. I fancy the new section, the Timber Corps; they're calling them the Lumber Jills," replied Jo, *"my mother thinks like yours and wants to see me cooped up in an office. I couldn't stand getting stuck as a secretary, typing and filing useless bits of paper for a lot of men...The Jills get to cut down trees, drive tractors and saw up the wood in mills. Proper work."*

"Actually, that's a coincidence. You do know Penny, I think. From up Harcombe Farm, where we've walked to from the river and scrounged some eggs."

"Yes, I remember her, she's a real Dorset farmgirl, if ever there was one," Jo responded.
"Well, she's actually exempt, working on the farm, but she applied to the Women's Land Army anyway. Apparently, because she passed her matriculation exam at school, they're putting her in the Women's Timber Corps. She showed me her papers. Off to Suffolk for training."
"Wow, I'm really envious...However, we've a few years to wait. We're over the school-leaving age, 14, but you have to be about 17 to join, I think," Jo muttered slightly sullenly. But then, brightening up, *"In the meanwhile, we've got our GIs to get to know a bit better. They're like us...strangers...outsiders...and away from home. That's the plus bit. My father's away. He's a still a POW after his bomber was shot down in one of the Lancaster bombing raids over Germany. We think he's now in Stalag Luft VI.*[7] *Been moved recently. It's way up nowhere in some place called Heydekrug, I think. Prussia, or somesuch. Mum's living with her sister in some cramped, crummy place back outside of Plymouth."*

Jo thought for a minute, then said, *"To get the GIs to really look at us, we'll have to make the most of the make-up we have. I've got a good powder compact and a scarlet lipstick...you've got some rouge and your eyebrow pencils. But, you're darker than me..."*

Ruth thought about this, then suggested, *"I think I can get my mother to send some of their spare cosmetics. She and her friends use quite a lot of make-up. It's probably after watching their favourite Jewish stars like Chaplin's wife, Paulette Goddard. When you saw 'Modern Times' and 'The Great Dictator', did you know that she's really Marion Levy? Or that Hedy Lamarr's real name is Hedwig Keisler? There have been lots of Jewish women on the silver screen…including Mae West, Judy Holliday, Luise Rainer – she won two Oscars…I adored the 'Great Ziegfeld', and now we've got Lauren Bacall. She ought to be bigger than all of them."*

"That's good if we can share some more make-up," commented Jo.

"When we came to Lyme Regis first, you wouldn't have even considered make-up, Jo!"

"Well, I've changed my mind now."

"Changing the subject," Ruth interrupted, *"what about all the stuff we're getting bombarded with about VD at school at the moment?"* [8]

Jo responded, *"We had the Deputy headmistress, Miss Dynes, give us a talk. She was most awfully embarrassed. Told us that almost all the Americans have had sexual relations while in North Africa and Italy, and that she believed over five per cent have had venereal disease – VD – and she told us it is easy to get from what she called 'sexual touching'. Whatever that means."*

"James from my class gets to play darts and skittles round the pubs with his dad, who's on the lifeboat and a local bobby. He says that they're putting up VD posters in all the gents' lavatories. It shows a girl entering a doorway with a GI and the letter 'V' for victory has been crossed out, and 'VD' has been scrawled up in its place. He also told me that the Ministry of Health have set up a local clinic on Wednesday afternoons at Dorchester County Hospital – women at 3.30 p.m.; men at 4 p.m. Doesn't seem to allow a lot of time if there's a lot of customers!"

Jo was in one of her fairly determined moods: *"The local boys are boring, most of them smell, have spots and have no money or manners...the Yanks are good lookers and have plenty of money to spend...on us."*
"I was told that the GIs get their own US army issue condoms for free."
"Well, I don't know about you, Ruth, I reckon we've got to live a bit. We've already learned about death – your father in Poland, and both of us in Plymouth."
Ruth went quiet for some moments, then said, *"Coming from Poland originally, my mother has repeatedly told me that she didn't expect to get out. She thought she'd be targeted by the Nazis and killed."*
"Even more reason then. Let's live a bit. Get some experience of our own while we can."
"And even George Orwell agrees about the GIs we

have round here. Did you see what he wrote in the 'Tribune' then reported in our 'Observer' this week?"
"No," replied Jo.
"Orwell wrote that, 'The general consensus of opinion seems to be that the only American soldiers with decent manners are the Negroes'. "

* * * * * * * * * * *

At almost the same time, post-chow line at the Laundry Fields camp, Eugene, Franklin and some other GIs were also having something of a planning meeting.
"Well, corporal," said Franklin to Eugene, whilst taking a draw on his cigarette, *"it's our night on furlough tonight. We going up to one of the Limey pubs?"*
"We've got pass-outs until 11.30, as long as we're careful over the black-out. I think we're invited for this English game, darts, with some of the locals at the Royal Lion tonight, starting about 8 p.m., so perhaps get there for 7.30," Eugene replied. One of the other GIs chipped in, *"It must be safer than that zinc bath full of cider we collected from the Dolphin and brought back to camp...my stomach's still cramping up just with the memory. Never again."*

The American 1st Infantry Divisional command had been working its troops hard. Lots of night 'problems' – exercises – many involving long manoeuvres through difficult countryside and along the treacherous cliffs towards Bridport. So, it was a real sense of relief for the half a dozen black GIs to have an evening away from their army lives. The group arrived just before 7.30 p.m. at the Royal Lion. The old coaching inn was just a little way up from the sea and Cobb Gate, on the right-hand side of Broad Street. The entrance doorways were quite low, so the taller GIs had to duck their heads on entering. Eugene spoke quietly to his companions, *"Let's try not to get into any more practice wars, tonight. OK?"*

As they pushed open the swing doors into the hotel entrance of the Royal Lion, they were confronted by a hand-written sign on the next set of doors, which led to the left into the low-beamed bar. It read:

'For British people and coloured Americans only'

"Holy Cow...Goddam...What about that then boys? These locals sure do seem to make us right welcome round here."

As the GIs entered the ancient smoky bar room, one of the locals turned round from the bar and came towards them, cheerfully holding out his hand to shake:
"You know me, Jack the Gas, from the gasworks. Welcome to the Lion," and turning to Ernie, the short,

plump barman, *"put 'em up pints of best!"*
Eugene introduced his men and they admitted to the all-male locals that they'd only ever thrown darts a couple of times and didn't properly understand the rules. Eugene, Franklin and the others were a bit quiet at first, but the warm beer quickly loosened up their tongues and dart-throwing arms. Jack acted as an informal master of ceremonies and after explaining the rules of 501 darts with double-in, and double-out, let the GIs get in some practice. It was very obvious that they were going to be no match for the local, much older and skilled regulars.
"What we'll do," instructed Jack, *"is we'll play pairs, one of us with each of you Yanks. That should even it up a bit. Make a game of it. I think our lot better do the scoring,"* he added, taking up a piece of chalk and scrawling the names of half a dozen of the Dorset men, himself included, at the top of the blackboard used for scoring. Eugene told him the names of the six GIs and this prompted another round of handshakes and a pause in activities. It also gave Eugene the chance to buy a round for the dozen or so locals in the bar, which was loudly appreciated.

The doubles games commenced just after 8 p.m., and the GIs gradually got the hang of scoring doubles, trebles, bulls and subtracting their scores. But there was no way that they could match the mental speed of the Royal Lion regular dart-players, who knew arcane things like 97 being a triple 19 and a double-top to get out and win a game. By nine o'clock the number in the bar had swelled a bit with some new arrivals, who were duly introduced to the GIs. The GIs knew they had a lot more money than the locals and were happy enough to spend it, buying most of the rounds of beer that night.

A new game had just begun when there was an absolutely terrifying series of bangs and the sound of the glass window shattering in the front of the bar next to the dart board. Those in the bar instinctively dived down, covering their heads. There were cries and shouts of alarm: *"What the....?"* And then, just as suddenly, it was over. Dust filled the air and shards of broken glasses littered the tables and floor. Gradually, as everyone in the bar emerged from where they had thrown themselves in the melee, conversations re-commenced. An elderly local, retired butcher called George suggested:
"Must have been one of the German planes, probably a Messerschmitt, straffing the town. Didn't hear that bugger coming." In the distance, there was the sound of anti-aircraft fire.

"Here, come look at this," cried Jack the Gas, pointing at the dart board, *"look at the bull – bloody bullet's passed straight through the middle, by Christ!"* One

of the locals responded, yelling out, *"Ay-thang-yew,"* which broke the almost icy silence. The bar-room filled with loud, slightly hysterical laughter. *'Ay-thang-yew'* was currently a very popular catchphrase of the English comedian, Arthur Askey. It seemed an appropriately British response to a German air-raid!

No more dart-playing took place that night, but the camaraderie between the GIs and the locals was intense. Lots of back slapping, exchanging of cigarettes, more rounds of bitter and mild, and questions from the locals about how 'Bolero', the name for the invasion build-up, was going. The GIs dodged these with polite answers about it being 'classified'. However, ever one for 'business as usual', Jack the Gas took Eugene to one side, saying, *"I seen you park your PX ration wagon down in the gasworks...tomorrow come and see me in my office there, and we'll work on a little business proposition I got in mind. Might as well all make a bob or two out of this bloody war...I like to see myself as 'Jack be nimble, Jack be quick'...and get rich quick, at that!"*

Just on ten o'clock, those inside the Lion became aware of yet another commotion outside in Broad Street. A Lyme member of the Home Guard came crashing into the bar: *"Been to the cinema...old man Turner just stopped the film and announced to everyone that a German plane has been shot down and they're bringing in some of the crew in one of the air-sea launches."*

That was the end of darts night at the Royal Lion. Eugene and his group of GIs joined a throng of nigh on 200 adults and older children as they headed down to Cobb Gate and along the Marine Parade towards the Cobb harbour. The sentries on guard at either end of the Parade gave up, outnumbered and overwhelmed. As the crowd, or perhaps in reality, lynch-mob reached the Cobb, someone yelled, *"Give us the Jerries...Give us the murdering Huns."*

But just then the three bedraggled Germans were brought along the Cobb Wall from the rescue launch. One was on a stretcher, a second was being supported by two military personnel, and the third limped his way under guard towards a waiting ambulance. The enemy suddenly looked very far from being the Supreme Race. They were simply very young, extremely scared and obviously both humiliated and vulnerable. Some of the women turned their heads away. A few grabbed the arms of the men who had been yelling for the Germans' blood. The crowd started to shamble away. The people of Lyme Regis had seen very little of real Germans apart from on newsreels at the cinemas, and these particular Germans made the onlookers feel increasingly uncomfortable.

7.

Preparations and entertainments: 1943 into 1944

A member of the Home Guard

"At least one platoon night problem per week, which has produced excellent results as regards control, formation and aggressiveness. Bayonet training has been emphasized...Recreation facilities were plentiful and utilized to the utmost...Morale good, food excellent."

G.A. Taylor, Colonel, 16th Infantry
Commanding, 1-31 December 1943.

Jo was in a state of agitation and excitement, as was her friend, Ruth. There was to be a New Year's Eve special party and dance – a hop – organised by the local Lyme women in the Woodmead Halls especially to entertain the troops. With some help from the resourceful Mrs Green, Jo and Ruth had managed to secure tickets. And lots of their friends were going. *"I really fancy the Americans. They treat you different,"* Jo exclaimed to Ruth in their room at 'Lavenders'.

Ruth was busy trying on her dress, even though it was only mid-afternoon. She'd spent hours making it herself out of materials recycled from a sheet and curtain which Mrs Green had given her. Ruth had been taught to sew by her mother, Rebecka, and excelled at what they called 'Domestic Science' lessons at school. In ordinary language these were sewing and cooking. *"Do I look alright?"* she asked Jo, who replied, *"I'm sure you'll be one of the belles of the ball."* The next hours were a happy swirl, as the girls exchanged and applied make-up – Ruth's mother had come up trumps and sent some part-used cosmetics to add to their own meagre selection. They washed, arranged and then re-arranged their hair-dos. They practised walking in unfamiliar high-heeled shoes, borrowed for the occasion. Their lives were filled with the intoxication of dreams and eager anticipation.

Woodmead Halls was crowded to the gunwales. The local women organisers had enlisted the Home Guard to 'police' the event and a couple of their number were outside the entrance. The place was overflowing smoke, music and laughter out into the night. Jo and Ruth had plenty of dances and even more offers. It was all extremely raucous and almost impossible to speak and be heard. Very few local men were present, but there were plenty of women, ranging in age from about 14 to the elderly. The sedate ones sat at long tables round the edges of the hall, and a bar had been set up in the serving area, run by the landlord from the Angel Inn, just at the bottom of Woodmead Road.

About 200 GIs including officers and privates were packed into the hall. The white troops vastly outnumbered the coloureds and there was no mixing. The white GIs were very obviously the noisier group. The coloured soldiers kept to themselves a lot of the time and were less 'forward' in inviting the women and girls to dance. In fact, it was the women who were doing most of the 'asking'. The band was playing popular dance tunes – a lot of dance and jiving numbers like 'Lindy Hop', 'Jitterbug Jive' and 'American Patrol' – so the hall was hot and sweaty with the tang of beer and cider and the fug of tobacco smoke. Most of the Dorset and Devon locals had never before seen the lindy hop, jitterbugging and jive performed in such an exuberant way. When the band performed Cab Calloway's 'Jumpin' Jive', two pairs of GIs gave a superb demonstration of superhuman dancing which was straight out of a Hollywood film! They tap danced, they jumped, they did the splits. This was not your average Dorset night at the Woodmead Halls.

'The jip-jam-jump is a jumpin' jive
Makes you nine foot tall when you're four foot five!'

Jo had already asked Franklin Harden, one of the coloured privates, to dance three or four times. As the 'bells' of midnight approached they were chatting together in the entrance area. A couple of white GIs roughly barged into Jo and Franklin, banging him into the wall. The taller one snarled, right up against his face: *"What are you nigger boy trash doing with a decent white girl...we'd be stringing you up back in Texas."*
The shorter and much stockier GI smirked, *"The likes of you black trash is only any good for doing the Jim Crow dance."* [9] This had become the symbol of slavery and segregation in America's southern states. The song and dance had been popularised by a minstrel show performer, Thomas 'Daddy' Rice back in the 1820s and the song was a mockery of a black, disabled slave's awkward and jumpy rhythms, dancing to the words of the song:

'Weel about and turn about and do jis so,
Every time I weel about I jump Jim Crow.'

Jo grabbed hold of Franklin's arm and moved him outside, saying, *"Let's get away before there's real trouble."* The two white GIs swore loudly still chanting, *"Jim Crow, Jim Crow,"* but luckily for the couple, didn't follow. Looking back, Jo saw that two of the Home Guard were now talking to the GIs and preventing them from following the couple. Franklin found himself guided by Jo to the back of the halls. It was a bitterly cold night, and their breath made clouds in the near-midnight air. Jo continued to steer Franklin into the darkness of a doorway to an outhouse, away in the corner of parking area. *"Come here,"* Jo mouthed quietly, pulling Franklin against her and starting to undo the buttons of his long coat. Franklin happily agreed and his body took on a life of its own. Jo could feel his rigid penis pressed against her, whilst Franklin wrapped his coat right round her. The war had changed everything. Like so many others, they were very literally making the most of every moment.

The couple caressed each other, kissing with tongues, and more and more vigorous movements as their bodies instinctively sought comfort in each other. Franklin went to undo the buttons of his trousers, but instead Jo took over and held his erect and hard penis against her and fondled it, until Franklin came. He wasn't inside her, as he would have wished, but he didn't try to go further. He showed respect for her. He certainly didn't want to upset her. For her part, Jo was finding this adventure both filling her with excitement, but also some pangs of fear.

Jo let Franklin walk her the short distance back to 'Lavenders' and the couple enjoyed a last kiss at the gate to the house. Then, upstairs, Jo shared tales of the evening with Ruth, as Franklin, who was a bit loaded, weaved and wobbled his way down to the footpath by the little River Lim, and back along the riverside to his tent at Laundry Fields. Almost at the camp perimeter he was accosted by some very merry and extremely sozzled local lasses. They were loudly serenading the GIs who had already made it home, with their own version of the Cole Porter cowboy song, however they'd changed the words to:

"And turn me loose on my cayuse, But please don't fence me out!"

They then yelled and screamed: *"We want to say good-night to our sweeties,"* and *"We'll give you something to help you with the invasion!"*

8.

Sports Day

A US sergeant talking to an English police sergeant

The sergeant at the microphone yelled, *"Yowzer, yowzer, yowzer! And welcome to all of you. A big Uncle Sam welcome from the United States army to this, the First Lyme Regis All-American Sports Day."*

It was a Sunday early afternoon, after the end of the day's religious services. Hundreds of Dorset and Devon locals were crushed into every available space, spilling into the fields around the Lyme Regis Football Club's ground at the Davey Fort. The ground, a solitary flat area, perched to the right of the Charmouth Road, lies precariously above and below the unpredictable landslips of Black Venn.

For a couple of weeks prior, representatives of the US 16th regiment had been touring around Lyme Regis, meeting with the Grammar School Head of Physical Training, the Town Council, the Mayor, the local Football Club officials and an assortment of council bigwigs and so-called dignatories. This group included the slightly shady, Jack the Gas, who, much to his delight, found himself as local liaison officer in charge of the catering. Jack hadn't managed to persuade Corporal Eugene to get involved with developing 'under the counter' trade in the town, but he'd had plenty of luck with lots of other GIs.

The challenge for the Americans was to promote and organise an American-style sports jamboree. As in many other cities, towns and villages throughout England, the event was billed as a 'Salute the Soldier' fund-raiser. This was a National Savings campaign designed to raise funds for the armed forces as part of what was called the 'People's War'.[10] The Bridport and District target was £7 per head, enough to buy six Churcill tanks. The Americans even persuaded the Grammar School to train up some of the schoolgirls as cheerleaders, and a small team of army personnel assisted the PT Department in this task, together with offering boxing tuition to groups of the older boys. Alongside this, two US female staff helped the Domestic Science Mistress and her pupils in the creation of a reasonably authentic set of cheerleader uniforms and pom-poms. Some of the girls remained a bit worried about the shortness of their cheerleader skirts!

The US army GIs loved nothing more than their sports, and in particular, the 'three Bs': boxing, basketball and baseball. The locals in Lyme had already witnessed dozens of the American GIs enjoying their sports practices and events in the open areas around the three main camps. For the men, it fed their competitive urges and provided opportunities to excel. GIs who were members of the official 1st Division sports teams were provided with extra rations, extra showers, time off to train, and for the coloured troops it was the only part of American army life which gave them a chance to fully represent their country. Despite the fact that only one in ten of the GIs were black, more than half of the boxing and basketball team members came from their ranks. At the national level, earlier in the year, a baseball pitcher's mound had even been installed in Wembley Stadium for a baseball game between two US service teams.

Ricky and his friends were amongst the throng at the Davey Fort ground. So too were Jo, Ruth and all the other members of the Lavenders' extended family. The Greens were there. In fact, only those too frail or not wanting to be part of the crush, had failed to be intrigued by the spectacle on offer. Two local police 'bobbies' were outside the ground and there were a few US guards around the sportsfield. They even used the opportunity to chat together, though the policemen looked strangely incongruous next to the GIs. On the way into the ground there was Jack the Gas, lording it in true proprietorial style, with GIs

cooking hot dogs – US issue frankfurter sausages. *"Come on, folks, step this way. Luverly American grub. Come on up. What are you a waiting ferr?"*
Jack had strapped on a big leather bag; more like a saddle bag, and was in charge of sales!

Originally hailing from Philadelphia, George S. Marks had come down to Lyme to help organise the sports day. Marks had a superb 16-3 win-lose record at baseball with his Philadelphia State Association back in 1940. In England he was as a US army athletic director. He organised four baseball leagues, a softball league, staged weekly boxing shows, plus putting on swimming galas and golf tournaments. In 1943, Marks was quoted in the 'Stars and Stripes' saying, *"Our aim is to offer opportunities for every soldier who wants to take part in athletics to do so. We are trying to keep the boys on duty, fit, alert and out of the pub and to an extent I think we are succeeding."* On this day, Marks succeeded in getting his 'boys' to work up a considerable thirst!

The first event of the afternoon was a basketball match between two of the best teams from the 1st Infantry Division. To the Lyme locals, the men seemed improbably tall, fast and agile. There was plenty to cheer and the match itself made English football look very slow by comparison. For the GIs taking part, it was a superb chance to show off American prowess to the Limeys. It was certainly working for the school-aged members of the audience. They cheered and roared on their support for the two teams. It was a great display, and after half an hour the score ended at 12-14, with an all-black team from the Supply Corps taking the laurels.

The Lyme Regis Town Band now played some tunes. Their versions of 'Land of Hope and Glory' and 'There'll always be an England' were predictable crowd pleasers. This musical interlude allowed time for the basketball hoops and stands to be taken down and a portable pitcher's mound to be set up. Plenty of polite applause thanked the local bandsmen. But they were quickly upstaged as a group of American bandsmen paraded onto the ground, and produced a much livelier set of Glenn Miller swing tunes including 'Little Brown Jug', 'In the Mood', 'Moonlight Serenade' and '7-0-5'. Their set had the locals and Americans up and dancing. By this time, the Football Club bar was open for business and was doing a roaring trade. Collecting buckets did the rounds among the spectators, raising funds for the 'Salute the Soldier' campaign.[11]

Ruth, Jo and a half a dozen other girls from the Grammar School now had to change into their cheerleader outfits to add some real American glitz into the baseball match. At just before 3 p.m., the American master of ceremonies returned to the ground. *"Yowzer, yowzer, ladies and gentlemen...For your delight and enjoyment, today we have assembled two teams to introduce you to the skills and excitement of our game of baseball. But since this little soccer ground is a mite small, we'll be playing softball, which has been a life-saver for our troops in your country."*

"And first let me welcome the cheerleaders...if baseball is as American as apple pie, these are some of the finest apples; young ladies picked for their good looks from your very own local High School...Give them a big, rousing welcome." And the crowd did indeed welcome them with a big cheer and lots of clapping. The girls were all dressed in similar costumes, bright red pleated sports skirts with tight white tops, braided hair and clutching black and red pom-poms. They'd had only a little time to practise and never in front of more than half a dozen spectators. But they were plucky and Jo and Ruth took their places in a line. Waving their pom-poms in either hand, the girls stood astride then jumped, arms whirling while chanting:
"Go boys go
Go give us a show
Hit that ball real hard
Go boys go!"
The two teams entered the main sports ground and the

girls repeated their cheers, while jumping up and down in a performance of organised, exaggerated excess.
"Go boys go. Go give us a show."
Over the Tannoy system, the sergeant MC informed the crowd, *"You're in for a real treat today, folks. George Marks, a pro-baseball player from Philly is leading the Reds, and another George, George Axelrod, a pro-player from New York City will lead the Blues. Give the boys a Big Am-er-i-can Cheer! Yowzer!"*

The crowd had been moved back to the field edges of the football ground but it was still really too small an arena even for softball. And dangerous for the audience too. The batters attempted to hit home-runs well into the back of the spectators' areas, while the pitchers took turns to look impressive on the home-made, wooden 'mound'. The cheerleaders kept shaking and waving their pom-poms and cheered alternately for the Blues and the Reds. But the crowd were not as impressed as their American hosts had hoped they would be. One of Ricky's school-mates told him, *"It's just rounders for grown ups."* Quite a lot of the adults drifted in and out to the bar, which continued to dispense copious quantities of mild, bitter and local farm cider. And in his corner of the ground, Jack the Gas continued to coin it in, selling the tasty but flaccid frankfurters in long bread rolls. He even had American mustard to accompany his fare.

The weather had blessed them with an unseasonally dry and warm day. The final event was the boxing. A makeshift boxing ring was set up in the middle of the ground and the sergeant informed the crowd that four fights were to be featured on the bill. The first three featured men stationed in Lyme.

Ricky, watching the second boxing bout found himself yelling hoarsely to his school mates:
"The white one, that's Sergeant Henry...I've told you all about him and his squaw up at Devondore."
Sergeant Henry was pitted against one of Corporal Eugene's squad; a tall, young private called Benjamin Jenkins. Benjamin was half a foot taller than the sergeant, and was a good stylist, circling the ring and using his height and reach advantage to outflank the sergeant. His jabs were landing him points. But the sergeant had bullish strength and hated losing, especially to what he called facetiously, 'his nigger friends'.

The first round had ended up pretty much all square. The second was going Benjamin's way. The spectators were fired up. The noise, the shouting all round, was deafening. *"Cumon, Ben," "Kill him, Sarge."*

Sergeant Henry, his eyes blazing with hatred, came in flailing heavy, short-range punches to Benjamin's guts, and a sequence of rabbit punches to his kidneys. The referee tried to stop the sergeant, but he was having none of it. Benjamin hit the canvas. He made it up on a count of five. But he looked groggy. Henry sensed a wounded beast. Grunting, and muttering, *"Go down, or I'll fuckin' kill you,"* at his opponent, Henry landed a left uppercut, quickly followed by a left-right combination to the nose and right eye. Blood rushed down Benjamin's face as he stumbled towards his corner. The bell saved him. However, his corner threw in the towel. It was all over; the sergeant was a victor of the boxing ring, as he had been on the battlefields of Tunisia and Sicily. After the decision, he was carried aloft and out of the ring, accompanied by victorious cheers and triumphal shouts from white GIs and many of the locals in the crowd. Ricky couldn't stop himself from bathing in the reflected glory of knowing and bragging about Sergeant Henry to the friends around him.

The third bout was a lacklustre affair, with none of the animal aggression of the second confrontation. But it was the final event on the boxing stage that caused something of a sensation. A formidable white boxer entered the ring. He called out, *"I'm a major. Name of Major James F. Jackson. You may have heard of me. I fought Joe Louis just before the outbreak of the war. Who wants a chance to floor me?"*

The challenge startled everyone at Davey Fort. This was old-style boxing. The boxing of the fairground booths. A number of the GIs looked at each other, but there were no takers. The referee picked up a microphone and temporarily became master of ceremonies, *"Now gentleman, today's for the 'Salute the Soldier' appeal. There must be someone out there who fancies the chance to fight our major here. And I've just been told that the US army will put up a purse of fifty US dollars for the winner."*
Hesitantly, an air force officer from the Cobb Harbour Air-Sea Rescue Base put up his arm, *"I guess I'm bomb-happy, or plain stupid enough to give it a go."*
"Welcome Bud," the referee said, *"What's your name?"* as he separated out the ropes so that the air force man could enter the ring. He then addressed the referee,
"I'm Warrant Officer Maurice Hollis, sir."
"Well, Maurice, you and James here, get yourselves gloved up."

And then, amidst a cacophony of noise from the crowd, the two men touched gloves and began their one-on-one combat. They were both big men, well muscled and obviously at the peak of fitness. Both were white and in their mid-20s, with James Jackson, the darker and more tanned of the two men. The first round had each man testing out the other, as they circled around each other, doing little more than casual sparring. The spectators were restless, with shouts of: *"Get on with it," "Let's see some action," "Stop pussy-footing."*

Then, on the bell for the start of Round Two, Hollis stormed out of his corner and landed two crunching right-hand blows into the jaw of Jackson. Jackson was knocked hard into his own corner. He looked visibly stunned. This wasn't what he'd expected, least of all from a Limey aircraftman. Hollis took the initiative landing some more good body punches as Jackson remained leaden-footed. Holding Hollis back momentarily, the referee looked into Jackson's eyes to see if he was OK to continue. The fight resumed. Jackson tried to re-compose himself, making a huge effort to counter effectively. Sidestepping, he swung with a good left punch which crunched into Hollis's chin. But Hollis had his spirits up. The crowd could sense an upset. They could see that Hollis was fired up to beat Jackson. The GIs tried to rouse their man, as the Lyme locals went mad cheering on Hollis. The screams of the crowd were deafening. Then the bell sounded. It was the end of the round and on to the third.

Again, it was Hollis who charged out into the centre of the ring like some raging bull. But this time Jackson came out to meet him. The two big men crashed into each other, slugging it out, punch for punch. Both

Jackson's eyes had puffed up, with the right one in danger of closing up. In the midst of this exchange, Jackson appeared to head butt Hollis hard in his face – blood spurted from Hollis's nose. Both men launched mighty right-hand blows at each other's heads. Both landed. Real hard. They swung left-handed follow-up punches. Both were trying to finish the fight. The blows landed again, hard and with force. Now the crowd witnessed the unlikely spectacle of both men falling backwards, hitting the turf of Davey Fort simultaneously. The referee commenced the count, *"...three, four, five...six, seven, eight, nine, ten, OUT!"* It was a double knockout. The crowd went wild with yelling and shouting. The smaller members amongst them were in real danger of being crushed as the crowd surged round the makeshift ring. The two boxers were revived and Hollis and Jackson were awarded a draw and shared the fifty dollar purse. A hard-earned prize.

The pubs throughout Lyme enjoyed a great night of trade as Americans and locals shared tales of the day they had experienced together at the Davey Fort.

9.

The 16th Infantry regiment away from Lyme in spring 1944

A crater in front of the Royal Sands Hotel at Slapton

"NOTICE
The public are reminded that requisition took effect from November 16th, from which date compensation is calculated...[December 21st]*...from that date the Admiralty may at any time and without notice enforce their right to immediate possession. It is therefore essential that EVERY PERSON SHOULD LEAVE THE AREA BY DECEMBER 20TH."*

K.G. Harper, Ministry of Home Security,
11th December 1943.

This order to evacuate a triangular section of the South Hams affected 3,000 local Devon inhabitants, 750 families, shops, schools and churches and involved the handing over of 30,000 acres of rich agricultural land as a practice assault landing zone for the US troops. Along with all the residents, all farm animals and pets were removed before the occupation of the area as a practice war zone. The farm animals mostly had to be put up for sale at special auctions. Unfortunately, since so many animals were for sale at the same time, they fetched very low prices. Meanwhile, some cats and dogs crept back. Successive groups of American troops enjoyed the undemanding attention that the animals offered whilst their real owners sadly missed their pets.

It was on March 12th 1944 that Sergeant Henry's platoon found themselves utterly exhausted, dirty and surrounded by many men nursing a range of injuries. They were there along with the entire Combat team of Company K, billeted in a makeshift encampment on the edge of the hamlet of Strete. They had 'captured' Strete on 'green beach' during an amphibious landing exercise at Slapton Sands earlier in the day, having experienced a barrage of live fire from the beach-head. There had been a number of casualties.[12]

The sergeant was in a dark mood. He spat and addressed his team:
"That was a fuckin' shitting mess out there. No-one seemed to know what was going down...and old shittin' rust-buckets to guard us. All the armchair generals' been doin' is buck passing...men were given live ammo and used it without realising...lots of live mines on the beach...we were killing each other...the radio frequencies were all to cock...I even pulled one of our guys back out of the water by his dog tag."

In this mood, no-one was keen to be seen challenging the volatile sergeant. So, Sergeant Henry continued, *"We sure do know now what the LSTs we were on board really stand for – it sure ain't: landing ship (tank). More like – long slow targets. Four and half thousand tons of a lumbering disaster waiting to happen. Fuck 'em. Fuck 'em all...Jeez I heard that there's been 200 of our boys killed in 'friendly fire' in these Slapton 'problems'. You can see why some of our boys go over the hill."* [13]

Prior to this, the combat team had been on board USS Barnett, which had embarked from Weymouth on the March 8th. They had also had a narrow escape from a German submarine which had surfaced in Start Bay, right in the midst of the mass of ships and vessels of all kinds, including landing craft and the DUKWs – the amphibious, motorised vehicles that were both boats and land vehicles. There had been a considerable exchange of fire with many wounded and killed before the submarine slipped away back towards the French coast. During the landing exercise the shelling from the attack force, or perhaps a bomb from the accompanying air-strike, had wrought further damage to the well-known Royal Sands Hotel and led to a number of casualties. The sandy stretch of beach was pock-marked with bomb craters. The hotel had previously suffered when a farmer's dog called Pincher had set off a mine buried close to the building earlier in the war. It was not the only building in that area, known locally as the Hams, that was never to be repatriated with its rightful owners.

Some of Eugene's colleagues from the Supply Corps were there too, living in bell tents, acting as drivers and labourers in uniform, humping box after box of live ammunition amongst the maze of signs warning of 'Danger' and '5 miles an hour'. The coloured troops were almost entirely in non-combatant roles. As in Lyme, the black African-Americans had arrived in the South Hams to clear the land for the establishment of the camps and it was the first time that the local populace had ever encountered a black person. Eugene and his small group kept themselves apart from the white GIs as far as possible. On the way into a segregated mess tent they encountered one of the stray animals – a black dog, which wagged its tail hopefully.
"You're getting better treated here than us Negroes," Eugene spoke to the dog, with considerable feeling.

Officially, the exercise, referred to in army-lingo, as 'a problem' was described in successful terms by Colonel Taylor, the colonel commanding the 16th Infantry regiment, as:
"Landing assault began at 0830, March 11th with assault units hitting the beach. The problem got well

under way with all units landing on schedule and the town of Strete being taken in order. At 1245 hours, Sunday March 12th the troops were on their final objective and dug in, after which the problem ended."

* * * * * * * * * * *

Cheesefoot Head, Hampshire

Throughout the southern counties of England, the Americans were very busy in April and May 1944 laying on major, mass morale-boosting events for their troops. These events brought together members of the many US regiments which were located across the counties of Hampshire, Dorset and Devon. Large sections of the 16th Infantry regiment attended two very special events held in the setting of the natural amphitheatre at Cheesefoot Head, outside of Winchester.

Both were shrouded in great secrecy. The first, held in April, had Joe Louis, the world champion heavyweight boxing champion,[14] known as the 'Brown Bomber' as its major attraction. His personal war effort involved fighting a variety of boxers in a series of exhibition bouts for audiences of GIs and a few specially invited dignitaries. The black Supply Corps GIs suddenly had one of their own coloured boys as a hero, but it was still an anachronism. Joe Louis, like any other black man in America, couldn't visit most theatres or even many sports stadia, since they were very strictly segregated. And in England, his fights were in front of largely white spectators, including predominantly white GIs. The second Cheesefoot Head event in May was the largest and most closely guarded secret. The enormous, green bowl was crammed to capacity with soldiers. On arrival, they hadn't realised that they would be addressed by General Eisenhower in person, giving the US soldiers, and many of the allied troops, his final impassioned rallying call. This was later broadcast on the radio:

> *"Soldiers, Sailors and Airmen of the Allied Expeditionary Force! You are about to embark upon a great crusade, toward which we have striven these many months. The eyes of the world are upon you. The hopes and prayers of liberty loving people everywhere march with you. In company with our brave Allies and brothers in arms on other fronts, you will bring about the destruction of the German war machine, the elimination of Nazi tyranny over the oppressed peoples of Europe, and security for ourselves in a free world.*
>
> *Your task will not be an easy one. Your enemy*

is well trained, well equipped and battle hardened, he will fight savagely.

But this is the year 1944! Much has happened since the Nazi triumphs of 1940-41. The United Nations have inflicted upon the Germans great defeats, in open battle, man to man. Our air offensive has seriously reduced their strength in the air and their capacity to wage war on the ground. Our home fronts have given us an overwhelming superiority in weapons and munitions of war, and placed at our disposal great reserves of trained fighting men. The tide has turned! The free men of the world are marching together to victory!

I have full confidence in your courage, devotion to duty and skill in battle. We will accept nothing less than full victory!

Good Luck! And let us all beseech the blessings of Almighty God upon this great and noble undertaking."

General Dwight D. Eisenhower

Back in Lyme after the Eisenhower speech, Eugene reflected on what he'd heard. *'Hell,'* he thought, *'free men of the world...marching together to victory...I don't much feel free.'* Later in the night when he couldn't sleep, Eugene took out a sheet for writing home and began to compose a note to his parents in Dallas.

He began writing on the specially prepared US government V-mail slips of paper. He was careful to use capital letters in his neat handwriting. Eugene knew that every letter to and from troops was checked and censored. His letter-back-home would be checked by mail-censors, then photographed and transported as a thumbnail-sized image in negative microfilm, and printed out and delivered to his folks in the US.

> *'Dear Ma and Pa*
>
> *England is being good to me. These white folks are mostly good, kind people here. Far different to back home. I've made friends, even met a nice girl, Edith. You'd like her. The food is fine, so your boy's body is okay.*
>
> *But in this drear, early morning hour, my head feels fit to burst. Us colored boys thought that we were here to be part of winning this war with our allies. But here in our American army we're not included. We're in servitude.*

Still slaves, inferior, insignificant in a white man's war. We're still slaves, just because we were born American Negroes.

You remember how proud of me you were when I passed my major and minor in Mathematics and English respectively after three years in college. When I was at the Army Reception Center, I told them about those grades and my passes at high school. Now, as a soldier in the United States of America's army, I'm forced to stay in a labor battalion. We're good enough to dig latrines, shift boxes, march, salute, drive and wait on the white officers while they stuff themselves with the best food. But even to our faces we're called, "darkie, nigger, son of a bitch". We're a bunch of permanent K.P.s, and the white GIs in the 1st Division where we are staying, call us "...the nigger corps down on the laundry fields". Then, some of my own men, African-Americans like me, they think because I'm a corporal, that I've changed sides. I've even heard them call me, "Uncle Tom".

I must go now.

You know that I love you and all our family.

I miss you and I trust in Our Lord that I'll be back with you soon.

Yours truly, your son
Eugene'

10.

Other tales

An RAF vehicle crashed into a shop window in Broad Street

The local newspaper, 'The Bridport News' reported on just a few of the events which really mattered in the area during the time of the American 'invasion'. The number of road accidents, sadly often fatal, increased alarmingly. Most involved military vehicles but the outcomes were put down to 'misadventure'. Much of the time it was impossible to locate the vehicle or the drivers responsible, and where they did, as with an American jeep which injured a pedestrian in Bridport's South Street, it was reported as being caused by *"some unknown reason"*.

Mrs Tennant, a very experienced horse-rider from Beaminster was reported as having been in a collision with a *"large army vehicle just outside of Beaminster"*. She was killed. Likewise, on May 6th 1944, Gunner Robert Canington was found dead in East Road, Bridport. It was reported as *"a likely accident involving a military vehicle"*. Lack of driver experience, driving on the unfamiliar left-hand side on narrow roads, the heavily dimmed lights on vehicles driving at night, and lack of lights at all on many vehicles, coupled with the absence of road signs (to confuse any German parachutists), meant that many of the US vehicles were accidents waiting to happen. In Seaton one evening, a truckload of English and Canadian army and air force troops had been out partying. As they approached the bridge a group of GIs saw the truck veer into the bridge and tip over. It was hushed up, but the locals talked of 'five of our boys' being drowned, but the US GIs had dived in and saved quite a few. And in Lyme itself, an RAF vehicle went out of control and crashed into a shop below the Royal Lion Hotel. Altogether in March 1943 alone, there were 43 fatalities on Dorset roads, seven during blackouts, plus another 31 seriously injured.

But other wartime misdemeanours were not hushed up. Such was an occasion that involved Jack the Gas from Lyme. He'd been sailing close to the authorities' winds for some time. In fact in the autumn of 1943 he'd been down on Monmouth Beach to check out his open fishing boat. Mr Dexter came stalking over towards him. The harbourmaster was a rather nasty shade of beetroot.

"We can't be having this, Jack, you've been warned too many times before."

"What's the problem. John, I've known you for years, and you knows I just like to continue to catch a few fish nows and again."

John Dexter was a bit of a jobs-worth. His little military moustache quivered as he replied, *"Well you've done it one time too many on my watch. I'm reporting you for no permit and I saw that you hadn't properly immobilised your boat, neither."*
"Fuck off, John, you're just a jumped up toe-rag. You'd be good in the Gestapo."
"That's it Jack. You're for it now. I'm getting Special Constable Bury down here. Now. This very moment. You're for the high jump."

Two months later, Jack found himself on the same magistrate's court bill as his friend, Mavis Curtiss. She was the stewardess at the Harbour Club, down on Monmouth Beach, which ironically served mostly the air force personnel. They both ended up in the 'Bridport News'. Mavis was found guilty of allowing a light to be shown at the rear of the premises during blackout. She was fined £2 with two shillings and six pence costs. Jack got clobbered a fair bit harder. It was reported that Jack was *"guilty of navigating a boat in tidal waters without a permit from naval authorities"*. He was fined only £1, but with £3 14s 6d costs against him, plus an additional five shillings fine for failing to immobilse his boat. Harbourmaster John Dexter allowed himself to puff out his chest in pride at successfully fulfilling his civic duty. Jack winked at Mavis as they left the courtroom and invited her out at the weekend for a few drinks to celebrate. Typical of Lyme humour!

However, Jack consoled himself with the knowledge that he'd sold over fifty quids worth of mackerel 'under the counter' to Lyme's one and only fish merchant in the past three weeks alone. Given that Lyme was woefully short of fish supplies, he'd even managed to get the fishmonger to give him three shillings and six pence a stone for the fish, which was thruppence over the maximum permitted price. But the authorities hadn't caught up with 'Our Jack' for that one! And they had completely failed to spot Jack's blossoming meat trade which he'd managed to incorporate into his task of 'testing out' the US vehicles after repairs had been carried out at the Gas Works. On these little jaunts to inland farms, with names like Hog Farm, Silverknowes and Knapps' Drop, Jack would collect whole sides of beef, butchered pigs and lambs and deposit them surreptitiously at the two Lyme Regis butchers. *'Now,'* thought Jack, *'that really was a nice little earner.'*

Jack was a one-man economic miracle, 'oiling' the local Lyme economy. He sold meat and fish, and exchanged goods for cigarettes, or other scarce American food and fancy items like ladies' nylon stockings, especially with his new US mate, Fred the Chef at the Three Cups. He also did a thriving trade with the officers at The Chalet and the Old Monmouth Hotel.

It was now the Saturday night when Jack was due to meet up with Mavis from the Harbour Club for a few drinks post their court appearances. They arrived pretty much at the same time as planned at 7 p.m. in the Royal Lion Hotel, Jack's preferred 'local'. On meeting, he pecked Mavis on the cheek and gave her a pair of nylons. *"You can thank our American friends for these, Maeve."* Jack got in drinks for the two of them and they found seats in a corner over by the heavily blacked-out windows facing onto Broad Street. The Royal Lion also doubled as the Home Guard HQ which Jack had joined. He told Mavis, *"You know I'm in the Home Guard. We go up Devon Point on the cliffs, stand watch. And instead of breaking radio silence, we run back down here to the Lion to give information to our HQ, and if we're lucky, have a quick pint. I do right well with my free trade with the Home Guard lads. Keeps the home fires burning, so to speak."*

At this moment Edith who works in the Marine Theatre NAAFI came into the bar.

"Hi Mavis, hi Jack. How's it going?"

"Come and join us, Edith," replied Jack, *"plenty of room for all. What you drinking?"*

"Thanks, Jack, I'll have a half of shandy, please."

Jack got up and went over to the bar which was pretty busy, it being a Saturday night and lots of soldiers had passes.

"Well then, Edith, how's it going with that American fellow of yours?"
"Eugene, you mean? He's fine. I like him. Really kind. Quiet and a bit reserved unlike a lot of the white, southern lot. And he's right well educated too."
Mavis looked round to see who was listening, then whispered to Edith, *"You know I live down in Coombe Street. Well you've never in all your days seen such things as I have recently. All along the fencing by the Laundry Fields camp, used rubber johnnies hanging like's they were on a washing line. Then, down near me in the square round Monmouth Street – Cats' Park we call it – I saw one GI running out of a house there with just his pants on. The woman's husband had come home and caught them at it!"*

Edith looked over and spotted that Jack was still waiting to get served at the bar, and whispered back, *"The women round here have gone bonkers and the older ones seem even worse...them's with their husbands away or working, they've got to putting a broom outside their doors when they're available. It's not even as if they were prostitutes, they're just making the most of it...it's just one mass shag."*
Mavis looked round a bit guilty, and then replied, *"I have to say I've been making a fair bit of hay while the sun's shining. A right pick and mix I've been having. But I've been a bit worried by all the talk of the clap,*

gonorrhoea, so I went for a check-up over Dorchester. But touch wood, it came back negative. Thank God!" [15]

Jack rejoined the ladies at this point, bringing with him the shandy for Edith and more drinks for Mavis and himself.

"So, what are you ladies chatting about?"

The ladies blushed a bit and Mavis said, *"None of your business, Jack, and you be keeping those roving hands of yours to yourself. I know you of old."*

11.

A furlough away to Teignmouth

Cannington Viaduct, between Lyme Regis and Axminster

"AT HOME in America you were in a country at war. Since your ship left port, however, you have been in a 'war zone'. You will find that all Britain is a war zone and has been since September 1939. All this has meant very great changes for the British way of life...But more important than this is the effect of war itself. The British have been bombed, night after night and month after month...Sixty thousand British civilians – men, women and children – have died under bombs, and yet the morale of the British is unbreakable and high."

Excerpts from the 1942 US War and Navy Departments' publication, 'A Short Guide to Great Britain'.

Jo and Franklin were sitting together, holding hands and enjoying their drinks in a quiet corner of the Dolphin pub. Landlady, Ma Bowditch didn't hold any truck with stopping so-called 'under-age' lasses and lads into her public house. As long as they toed the line and behaved like her adult customers.

"Tell me about your time in Plymouth, Jo," Franklin prompted.

"Well, you know, I was at Dame Alleyn's School; my friend Ruth was there too. My dad and mum had married before the Depression-time, back in the twenties. They'd met while my dad was still at university in London, when he was back on vacations. He was doing research in town planning or something and got a job with Plymouth Council. We lived in a nice house, then came the drone of the bombers coming over the city and the fires that never seemed to be put out. There was the awful wail of the sirens sending us scurrying to the public air-raid shelters.

I still wake up in the night with the sound of those sirens in my head. We had played in Victoria Park. Then came the bombs. The bandstand where we played was totally destroyed. Smoke, fire-engines, wardens ordering us about, more sirens, the almost ever-present gas and huge big bomb craters everywhere."

"Wow, Jo, that sure sounds pretty awful...When did you leave?"

Jo took a large sip of her beer shandy and a drag on her cigarette.

"In 1941, dad was moved into active duty with the

RAF. And almost at the same time, March 1941, Plymouth got clobbered. Just about every night there were fearsome raids. My mum decided that we wouldn't use the public shelters. Instead we hid under the beds and tables, or down in the cupboard under the stairs. The centre of Plymouth was being ripped apart. It got worse and worse throughout March and April '41. And on the night of the 21st April 1941, that was when Plymouth was 'Coventrated', as we called it, just like poor old Coventry. Our house copped it and my mother decided to have me evacuated. She sorted it out with my school."

"Do you want another drink, Jo?" Franklin could see that re-telling her story had caused a wave of distress. *"Yes please, Franklin, that would be nice,"* Jo replied, dabbing away a few tears from her eyes. When Franklin returned from the the small bar after sharing a quick joke with some regulars, he said, *"I've had a letter from my brother, Lester. It turns out that his navy outfit has been moved to Teignmouth, down the coast, west from here. He wants me to visit him on my next furlough. It would be great if you could come. Fancy asking Mrs Green?"*
"Of course, that would be great, but I don't hold out much hope," Jo said.

Franklin's furlough came through for the weekend after

next, and, as expected, Jo was not allowed to join him on a trip down to Teignmouth. Nor was Eugene able to organise leave even though he was an old friend of Lester's. Jo was pretty grumpy the next time the two met up, but Franklin bought her some nylons and a supply of goods from the PX store, so she soon cheered up and gave him 'extra cuddles'.

Franklin hadn't used the English trains on his own before, so was a bit anxious about making the journey from Lyme's railway station up to Axminster on the steam train. He had been told that he had to change trains there for the trip to Exeter Central, with a further change for the final leg of the journey along what was known as the Riviera Coast to Teignmouth. For the furlough he'd obtained travel passes for the Friday until the Sunday when he had to be back at camp. He was greatly looking forward to seeing his slightly older brother, Lester. They had last seen one another back home in Dallas. So, it was time to play catch-up on each other's lives.

What Franklin thought of as his 'Furlough-Friday' came around at last. He found himself a place in a carriage on the early morning 8.08 a.m. train out of Lyme Regis and stored his kit-bag in an overhead rack. The three carriages were filled with small compartments with sliding doors, entered from a narrow corridor on one side. The whistle blew, and Franklin, crammed into his small compartment box with seven other people, including other US GIs, felt the train judder slowly forward. A billow of thick smoke from the steam engine at the front poured past them, with some sweeping in through the partly open carriage window. *"Get that sodding window shut,"* another passenger yelled, and Franklin who was sitting by the door, leant over and slammed the window shut.

Franklin, on his first short twenty minute journey on the local branch-line to Axminster, issued an appreciative, *"Jeez!"* as the train travelled across the Cannington Viaduct on its way to Combpyne Station, located fairly close to the famous Victorian Dowlands landslip of 1839. Franklin was treated to a brief history lesson about the event from another passenger, who informed him that, *"The landslip was incredibly well reported in the national newspapers, especially by the scientist William Buckland, who'd been in the area at the time. Thousands flocked down to Lyme to see the result. Goat Island, a fifteen acre outcrop of the local farmer's field was left isolated from the rest of the undercliff. The farmer charged the visitors a scandalous sixpence a head to visit the landslip area."*

The train continued its meandering way via the woods and hills of Shapwick, Trinity, Hartgrove and Trill along the route into Axminster. After waiting for the Waterloo-Exeter train, Franklin thought that the next stage of his train journey was far more bland, even though the countryside was growing green with the onset of spring. But better was to come. The third and final leg by train from Exeter Central to Teignmouth was an enchanting trip. Franklin found himself observing the Exeter canal and then the wide expanse of the Exe estuary, heavily encrusted with barbed-wire, then on the right-hand side of the carriage, the herds of deer in the Powderham Castle grounds of the Earl of Devon's estate. But best of all were the final stages of the journey where the railway line edged along the sea walls between Dawlish Warren and Dawlish town stations and then again to Teignmouth, after cutting through a series of red sandstone tunnels. Franklin couldn't resist telling his companions on this part of his journey that the views were, *"Just awesome."*

Lester had booked Franklin into simple lodgings in the RAF Roundel Club, just opposite the Teignmouth Station, on the corner of Station Road. The club even had a bar, so Franklin treated himself to a beer and chatted with Cyril, the bar steward. Cyril was indeed very chatty.

"Well Franklin, this war has been very hard for the people of Teignmouth. We're the most bombed town of our size in the whole of the south-west of England.

We've had over 20 air attacks, over 200 houses have been destroyed and another 2,000 damaged, even our hospital with three nurses killed. In all, we've had nearly 80 dead and at least 150 injured." [16]

Franklin found himself learning more about bombing raids on the harbour and unsuccessful attempts to blow up the railway line. Cyril then explained how the Morgan Giles boatyard was prospering, through building the specialised Vosper-type motor torpedo boats. Finally he told Franklin about the coming of the US navy workshop in 1943, situated right next door to the Morgan Giles' yard on the Fishermen's beach. By the time Franklin had finished his beer and bought Cyil one, he was ready to make his escape, wishing Cyril a hasty 'goodbye'.

Franklin ventured down into town via the Triangle, a pleasant seating area for pedestrians wanting a break, and on past the water fountain. Further towards the seafront he found himself facing the Pavilion to the left of an open grassy area, which he later learned was called the Den. The Pavilion area was a hive of activity. Dozens of American naval seamen and officers flowed in and out of the building and over onto the Den, where a full-scale baseball game was in progress. It amused Franklin to see the hitter with a fat cigar in his mouth as he prepared to take a strike. Franklin strode over to the

Pavilion. As a black man in his GI's uniform he didn't look too far out of place. At the door he saluted a naval lieutenant,
"Sir, I'm looking for my brother, he's a petty officer. Name of Lester Harden."
"Yes, I know Lester. He's billeted in the Quonset huts just over there by the Courtenay Hotel." The officer pointed Franklin towards the semi-circular metal huts a little way off the edge of the Den. *"Or, he could be inside the Pavilion here. This is our mess. Cookhouse is next door round the back of the bowling green."*
"Thanks, sir, I'll take a look for him inside if that's OK."

Going inside the Pavilion, Franklin was immediately confronted by a wall crammed full with large paintings of semi-nude women. They were pin-up style, idealised icons, and one had an earring attached, constructed from a crystal drop misappropriated from the chandelier hanging in the centre of the room. Dozens of men were chatting, smoking, drinking mugs of coffee and in one group to his right, Franklin spotted Lester.
"Hiya Lester, it's your kid bruv."
Lester's face was made for smiling and he grinned from ear to ear at the sight of Franklin. He bounded over, grabbing Franklin in a bear-hug, literally lifting him off his feet.
"Let me look at you...You sure done some growing.

You were hardly out of diapers last time I looked on you." Lester then added, *"You found your billet OK?"*
"No problem. I just escaped from Cyril, the steward there. He was trying to tell me the entire wartime history of this little town."
"I've managed to get today and tomorrow off. Back to the base on Sunday morning. But let me show you round." Lester ushered Franklin over to the table where he had been sitting.
"These are some of my buddies...meet Franklin, boys."
It was interesting for Franklin to see that this was a mixed group of seamen, both white and coloured. One of the older men held out his hand and shook Franklin's rigorously: *"J. Michael Turner's the name. If you ever need a first class funeral home in Emporia, Kansas, I'm your man."* Franklin couldn't help but smile back in bemusement.

A few minutes later, Lester led Franklin out of the Pavilion. *"I'll take you for a stroll round. Give you a chance to get your bearings. We've not been here long, but Teignmouth folk have made us welcome and there's plenty of good looking Devon girls. They speak a strange kind of English...call you 'my lover' and 'my handsome'...We'll have to see if we can set you up. I've got a date with one of our local bar-ladies from the Pavilion tonight. Been seeing a lot of her. She's great. We call her Dawn of the Den! You'll meet her*

later. She's just a bit younger than me...about twenty, I think."
Franklin looked a bit awkward and said, *"Actually I'm dating a girl in Lyme Regis where my unit and part of the Big Red One are based. She's called Jo. I'm getting pretty sweet on her, so I don't know..."*
"That's OK bruv...see how it goes, or how the 'cookie crumbles,' as these Limeys say."

Lester led Franklin past the Courtenay Hotel and just round the corner by the Bella Vista he showed him the massive electronically controlled rocket launcher. An impressive piece of kit. They next went down onto promenade and gazed out at the beach which had a long series of scaffolding poles mounted into the sand and covered in massive rolls of razor wire. It formed a formidable fence. However, people were still allowed on the beach between the prom and the defensive fortifications, but this being April, there were only a few hardy souls with their buckets and spades. Lester steered Franklin westwards along towards the Grand Pier and he told Franklin that Home Guard had dismantled a section of the pier as a precaution against a German invasion. This had isolated the farmost jetty and pavilion. Lester explained that his colleagues had devised a solution so that the troops could use the pier ballroom for dances. *"Us guys in the 28th Naval Construction Batallion – that's the 'CBs' – and why we're now known as the 'seabees'. We're the naval builders and craftsmen. So, we've made up our own temporary ramp system. Now we can get to that darned ballroom whenever we want."* At the pier's end, Franklin could make out a bofors gun and Lester told him there were two more further along the promenade, either side of the lighthouse.

As they walked westwards, still on Teignmouth's promenade, Lester pointed across the Den and the continuing baseball game. *"Our men are billeted in pretty much every hotel along the front; the Marina Hotel is our HQ. We'll go and take a look at US naval service area in a bit. Beyond the lighthouse, that's the Teign estuary. It's pronounced 'Teen', unlike the town, which they pronounce, 'Tinmouth'. Confusing, huh?"* He added, *"And that big red cliff face over the other side of the river is in Shaldon. It's called the Ness. This a pretty neat place. A far cry from Dallas. Hope you enjoy your little visit."*

At the Point, which juts out into the estuary at the far end of the promenade, Franklin found the substantial car park filled to the brim with military vehicles, plus an incongruously sited German plane. The local town council had put the plane there so that visitors could pay to view it and raise money for the war effort. The pair then turned right along the shore of the estuary and

into the working port area, known collectively as the Quays. Franklin got his first glimpse of the US naval area. Lester continued in his role as tour guide: *"We've gotten four service bays, mainly for servicing landing craft and a turntable for manoeuvrering the vessels we're working on."* But it was the strange array of what Franklin took to be floating barges, moored in the water beyond the service area, which caught Franklin's attention. *"What the devil are those, Lester?"*
"I'm not meant to tell you, really, but as you're military, I guess it's OK. They're being assembled here, ready to tow over as parts of a floating harbour for the invasion. Called mulberries, I been told."

That night Franklin was treated to a crawl round some of Teignmouth's many hostelries. They started at the far end of the narrow and quaintly cobbled, Teign Street. Lester persuaded Franklin to try a pint of local farm cider in the Blue Anchor. It was a cloudy red colour, which Franklin found a bit off-putting, but on tasting he commented, *"Hey, this is sure pretty good. Sweeter than the scrumpy I've tried back in Lyme."*
They didn't have far to walk to the next pub. The Teign Brewery is almost next door and it was where Lester had agreed to meet up with Dawn, who worked there as well as at the Den Pavilion. Sure enough, she'd been roped in by landlady Kay to give her a hand. *"Well, my handsome, what are you lads be wanting?"* Kay asked.

"I rather fancy Dawn if that's OK!" Lester quipped.
"She's been talking about seeing you for the last hour, but be warned, I reckon she'll be out-drinking the both of you. Hope you've got plenty of those luverly American dollars to spend on her."
Dawn called over, *"Mine's a red wine, Lester. Make it the good stuff, Kay!"* Franklin could see that both Dawn and Kay looked well capable of looking after themselves, but Dawn was a particularly striking young woman. A winning, open smile lit up her face, complemented with long blonde hair and a great, shapely figure. Franklin was well impressed with his older brother's choice. Lester ordered up a couple of pints of scrumpy, and wine for both of the young ladies. He then went about introducing Franklin to Dawn, Kay and some of the locals who were propping up the bar. They were a colourful lot. Men and women with 'lived-in' faces. Interesting characters who had very obviously experienced more than their fair shares of life's ups and downs.

Franklin couldn't help but notice that there was also a mix of white and coloured seamen in this bar. Indeed, four of them were playing an animated game of darts together.
"You all seem to get on pretty well together here, Lester."
By this time Dawn had come round their side of the bar

and answered for Lester. *"The US military did do the rounds of the pubs suggesting alternate nights for whites and coloureds, but like we normally do round here, Kay told them where they could go."* And Kay added, *"We don't see any trouble in here either. The lads wouldn't dare with us in charge! And then there's our dog. He's a Staffy and loves chasing guys in uniform."*

The night was a successful and boozy one. They visited at least half a dozen bars. The brothers dimly recollected the Devon Arms, the King Billy and the Lifeboat as being among them. Franklin and Lester ended the evening being propped up by Dawn. She had an arm around each of them as she steered them back towards the Roundel Club, where Franklin was helped up the steep stairs to his little bedroom on the first floor. He was very wobbly. As she left with Lester, she said to him, *"And I can see you're not fit for any hanky-panky, either."*

Saturday started slowly and somewhat blearily for both the Americans, but they hadn't planned anything until midday. Then, Lester took Franklin for a walk out of Teignmouth and across the heavily fortified Shaldon Bridge, so that his brother could have a look around Teignmouth's neighbouring 'sister' village. On the way over the bridge, Lester yelled to his brother, *"Look, down there..."* And following where Lester

was pointing, Franklin could see two tiny submarines. *"We call them the human torpedoes...they're midget submarines; just two men in each one."*
The whole waterfront at Shaldon was encased with high rolls of barbed-wire, with just one gap where the ferry plied its trade back and forth to Teignmouth. Right at the end of the village, near the mouth of the estuary, Franklin saw two very large naval guns located in front of the Georgian, Ness House. They ended their Shaldon visit with a ride back across the Teign estuary in one of the old Teignmouth ferry boats. The boatman proudly informed the brothers that his vessel, T&S2, had been built back in 1908.

That evening the brothers were scheduled to attend the weekly dance. This one was to be held at the Pavilion on the Den which served as the US naval mess and where the brothers had initially been reunited. A visiting US band was due to play, so everyone was really looking forward to it. The band's visit had been organised through ENSA, the British Entertainments National Service Association, working in co-operation with the American Theater Wing. Dawn had wangled the night off and she was bringing her friend Rachel along to keep Franklin company. The four met up not far from the Roundel Club, just at the end of French Street in the Kings Arms. Having recovered from the night before, Franklin and Lester both looked resplendent in their army and naval uniforms. The girls had made a real effort to look their best too. Dawn had put her hair up and applied just a hint of pink lipstick to match her dress, which adequately showed off her full bosom. Rachel was a tall, dark-haired girl, probably about the same age as Dawn. She was wearing a bright red dress with puffed shoulders. It soon became apparent that she was quiet and a bit shy with the two coloured Americans, but joined in a heated discussion Dawn was having with Lester about jazz music. The pub was already pretty full and very smoky even though it was only seven o'clock. All four contributed to the general fug by lighting up their cigarettes and trying to talk over the general hubbub.

Just on eight o'clock the group left the Kings and walked the short distance over to the Pavilion. As they arrived, the band started playing, so they congratulated themselves on their great sense of timing. Inside, couples were already well into the swing of the evening. The band was excellent with many coloured players who seemed to be able to seamlessly move from one rhythm to another. After they had found a table and ordered drinks, Dawn said, *"It's great not to be working here tonight. I tell you, I know just how tiring it is."*
And Lester, with mock-graciousness replied, *"Aw gee babe, it's great to have you here with me tonight. It's*

going to be a swell party."

To keep their table from being nabbed, the couples took it in turns to dance. The band were mostly playing Glenn Miller numbers and were going down a storm. In fact, Lester had heard that two of the band had actually played with Glenn Miller's military band, which had been formed in 1942 after Miller joined the army and was subsequently transferred into the army air force. All four enjoyed dancing and were really jiving to 'In the mood', not to mention 'String of Pearls' and 'Chattanooga Choo-Choo'. It was at about eleven o'clock when Lester and Dawn came back to the table, looking particularly flushed. *"Hey guys,"* Lester said, *"listen up. I've got an announcement. I've just told Dawn that I'm going to make an honest woman of her. Make her Mrs Harden, and gee, you know what, she's said yes. Let's make this one helluva party. I'm off to get us some champagne!"*

The champagne flowed and flowed and everyone had sore heads the following day. The worse for Lester as he was back on duty at eight in the morning. Franklin and Rachel enjoyed each other's company, but Franklin had been candid about his girl-friend back in Lyme, so they established a friendly understanding that this was an evening about companionship rather than anything more.

Sunday gave Franklin the opportunity for a last look around Teignmouth. He'd had to say his goodbyes to Lester and the ladies in the early hours of Sunday after they had spilled out of the Pavilion and onto the Den. The night had concluded with a riotous half an hour on the Den, when dozens of American condoms were inflated and kicked around in a surreal parody of a mass game of soccer. Dawn, Rachel, Franklin and Lester were more than sufficiently liquored-up to join in with the rest and got their dresses and uniforms rather muddy. Franklin smiled to himself at the memories of Dawn being carried around on Lester's shoulders, exuberantly waving an extra large condom and yelling, *"Look out, I'm Dawn of the Den!"* Rachel had got on his shoulders and they'd then had a good old condom piggy-back fight, but Lester and Dawn had outflanked them, and with one wild swing of her condom, Dawn had sent Rachel flying off Franklin's back, ending up in a muddy puddle. Franklin thought, *'It's great to be alive.'*

Travelling back on the scenic railway line to Exeter, he had some pangs of regret at leaving Teignmouth, but he also had some very happy memories of the place, his brother and the people he'd met. He was also hoping that if he got back early enough he'd be able to catch up with Jo.

12.

The last days in Lyme: the run-up to D-Day

LST 289 arrives in Dartmouth after Exercise Tiger

Overall, the months between New Year's Eve 1943 and May 1944 had passed very quickly for the American troops and the residents of Lyme. The regiment was no longer solely training in, or even located close to, Lyme. Lengthy exercises, practising amphibious landings took place at Braunton in Devon and other locations. The tension amongst the men was almost visible. They were experiencing a roller-coaster mix of emotions, encompassing dread, fear and excited anticipation. They knew that they were close to the time of the invasion, they just didn't know exactly when and where, and whether their regiment would be at the front of the action.

Franklin met Jo whenever he could, since despite the rigorous training regime, there was time off when the troops were back in Lyme. And Franklin learned more of the ways and wiles of a young English girl, and Jo discovered much about Americans, and one black American in particular. Together they went on walks along the footpaths following the little River Lim, up in the bluebell woods above the Spittles, and picnicked on the field known locally as the 'Bumpy', below the Grammar School. Jo felt that she was existing in some sort of make-believe bubble. They also found plenty of uses for Franklin's overcoat to cover both the ground and themselves as they explored each other's bodies.

One day early in May, Jo found Franklin very quiet and strangely morbid. She asked him if he was fearing the invasion. Franklin hesitated in answering, then after a good few moments, replied, *"Things have just gone badly wrong in the training. We lost a lot of men, we don't even know how many. Hundreds, maybe towards a thousand. They were training further west, practising landings and the German e-boats, Schnellbootes – the motor torpedo boats got them. Many of our men didn't even know how to inflate their Mae Wests, nor did they understand how to use the carbon dioxide belts they'd been issued with...one of our guys told me they couldn't get the lifeboat free and had to shoot off the release cable...many were burned alive in the oil-fuelled flames which engulfed the water around the sinking vessels...men were screaming, shouting and praying. I've heard that bodies have been washed up in Lyme Bay and as far away as Portland. That exercise was called 'Tiger' – our battalion had been involved in a similar one, same place, back at the beginning of March...the men on base have started calling it the*

'Night of the Bloody Tiger'."
Jo couldn't think of anything fitting to say in response. She pulled him into the warmth of her body and held him there. Their relationship was such that they both felt very, very content when they were together.

Following the disastrous Exercise Tiger, Franklin and the Services of Supply Corps and the 16th Infantry regiment, 1st Division were the lucky ones, but morale was badly affected. They were safe in Lyme in May 1944, with comparatively few scrapes, casualties and injuries, and some useful and relevant training under their collective belts. But the tension was ratcheting up. It was a time when many of Franklin's comrades in arms were thinking back to the rout that the supposedly invincible American troops had suffered from Rommel's troops at the Kassine Pass in Tunisia a little more than a year before. In that engagement the mass of American GIs had thrown down their rifles and run for their lives. Perhaps realising that 'Tiger' had seriously undermined troop morale, the American authorities felt they needed one last major pep-talk to fire them up in readiness for the assault on the beacheads of France.

Amidst great secrecy, General George Smith Patton was flown into England in January 1944. Despite being the best known American general, both feared and respected by the German High Command, Patton was meant to behave like a proverbial 'ghost'. His job was to appear to the Germans to be commander in charge of the First United States Army Group (FUSAG). This entirely fictitious army was created purely to fool the Germans. It consisted of dummy tanks, trucks, army camps, installations and airfields scattered throughout the south-east of England. They were supposedly being prepared for an invasion of France across the shortest possible route to Pas de Calais, as a major offensive in Operation Fortitude South.

February 20, 1944
Letter from George Smith Patton to his wife, Beatrice Patton:

> *'Yesterday I went into Butch's room and ran into the whole press, so I just told them I was a ghost and they admitted every one in town had seen me, no one would admit it. I wish I could stop being incognito but really it makes no difference as I am a very apparent entity.'* [17]

March 6, 1944
Letter from George Smith Patton to Beatrice Patton:

> *'This damned secrecy thing is rather annoying particularly as I doubt if it fools any one. Every time I make a speech I have to*

> *say now remember you have not seen me – a voice crying in the wilderness.'*

Patton was the US army's hero. And the soldier's ultimate soldier. Away from Lyme, at a secret and secure army-base somewhere on Salisbury Plain, Eugene, Franklin and many others from the non-combatant Supply Corps joined the men of the Big Red One. In turn, they were joined by men from many other American regiments to see and hear Patton. On that day, he didn't disappoint.

Standing in front of the troops, Patton began (and continued) in a blunt, direct way, talking to the men in a style and language that they could understand. Or, as Patton told his nephew: *"You can't run an army without profanity; and it has to be eloquent profanity. An army without profanity couldn't fight its way out of a piss-soaked paper bag."* It was in many ways in stark contrast with Eisenhower's speech just days before. It was full of the rhetoric of war, spoken as American-soldier-to-American soldier.

> *'Be seated.*
>
> *Men, this stuff that some sources sling around about America wanting out of this war, not wanting to fight, is a crock of bullshit.*

Americans love to fight, traditionally. All real Americans love the sting and clash of battle.

You are here today for three reasons. First, because you are here to defend your homes and your loved ones. Second, you are here for your own self respect, because you would not want to be anywhere else. Third, you are here because you are real men and all real men like to fight. When you, here, every one of you, were kids, you all admired the champion marble player, the fastest runner, the toughest boxer, the big league ball players, and the All-American football players. Americans love a winner. Americans will not tolerate a loser. Americans despise cowards. Americans play to win all of the time. I wouldn't give a hoot in hell for a man who lost and laughed. That's why Americans have never lost nor will ever lose a war; for the very idea of losing is hateful to an American.

You are not all going to die. Only two percent of you right here today would die in a major battle. Death must not be feared. Death, in time, comes to all men. Yes, every man is scared in his first battle. If he says he's not, he's a liar. Some men are cowards but they fight the same as the brave men or they get the hell slammed out of them watching men fight who are just as scared as they are. The real hero is the man who fights even though he is scared. Some men get over their fright in a minute under fire. For some, it takes an hour. For some, it takes days. But a real man will never let his fear of death overpower his honor, his sense of duty to his country, and his innate manhood.

Battle is the most magnificent competition in which a human being can indulge. It brings out all that is best and it removes all that is base. Americans pride themselves on being He Men and they ARE He Men. Remember that the enemy is just as frightened as you are, and probably more so. They are not supermen.

All through your army careers, you men have bitched about what you call "chicken shit drilling." That, like everything else in this army, has a definite purpose. That purpose is alertness. Alertness must be bred into every soldier. I don't give a fuck for a man who's not always on his toes. You men are veterans or you wouldn't be here. You are ready for what's to come. A man must be alert at all times if he expects to stay alive. If you're not alert, sometime, a German son-of-an-asshole-bitch is going to sneak up behind you and beat you to death with a sockful of shit! There are four hundred neatly marked graves somewhere in Sicily, all because one man went to sleep on the job. But they are German graves, because we caught the bastard asleep before they did.

An army is a team. It lives, sleeps, eats, and fights as a team. This individual heroic stuff is pure horse shit. The bilious bastards who write that kind of stuff for the Saturday Evening Post don't know any more about real fighting under fire than they know about fucking! We have the finest food, the finest equipment, the best spirit, and the best men in the world. Why, by God, I actually pity those poor sons-of-bitches we're going up against. By God, I do.

My men don't surrender, and I don't want to hear of any soldier under my command being captured unless he has been hit. Even if you are hit, you can still fight back. That's not just bull shit either. The kind of man that I want in my command is just like the lieutenant in Libya, who, with a Luger against his chest, jerked off his helmet, swept the gun aside with one hand, and busted the hell out of the Kraut with his helmet. Then he jumped on the gun and went out and killed another German before they knew what the hell was coming off. And, all of that time, this man had a bullet through a lung. There was a real man!

All of the real heroes are not storybook combat fighters, either. Every single man in this army plays a vital role. Don't ever let up. Don't ever think that your job is unimportant. Every man has a job to do and he must do it. Every man is a vital link in the great chain. What if every truck driver suddenly decided that he didn't like the whine of those shells overhead, turned yellow, and jumped headlong into a ditch? The cowardly bastard could say, "Hell, they won't miss me, just one man in thousands." But, what if every man thought that way? Where in the hell would we be now? What would our country, our loved ones, our homes, even the world, be like? No, Goddamnit, Americans don't think like that. Every man does his job. Every man serves the whole. Every department, every unit, is important in the vast scheme of this war. The ordnance men are needed to supply the guns and machinery of war to keep us rolling. The Quartermaster is needed to bring up food and clothes because where we are going there isn't a hell of a lot to steal. Every last man on K.P. has a job to do, even the one who heats our water to keep us from getting the "G.I. Shits."

Each man must not think only of himself, but also of his buddy fighting beside him. We don't want yellow cowards in this army. They should be killed off like rats. If not, they will go home after this war and breed more cowards. The brave men will breed more brave men. Kill off the Goddamned cowards and we will have a nation of brave men. One of the bravest men that I ever saw was a fellow on top of a telegraph pole in the midst of a furious fire fight in Tunisia. I stopped and asked what the hell he was doing up there at a time like that. He answered, "Fixing the wire, Sir." I asked, "Isn't that a little unhealthy right about now?" He answered, "Yes Sir, but the Goddamned wire has to be fixed." I asked, "Don't those planes strafing the road bother you?" And he answered, "No, Sir, but you sure as hell do!" Now, there was a real man. A real soldier. There was a man who devoted all he had to his duty, no matter how seemingly insignificant his duty might appear at the time, no matter how great the odds.

And you should have seen those trucks on the road to Tunisia. Those drivers were magnificent. All day and all night they rolled over those son-of-a-bitching roads, never stopping, never faltering from their course, with shells bursting all around them all of the time. We got through on good old American guts.

Many of those men drove for over forty consecutive hours. These men weren't combat men, but they were soldiers with a job to do. They did it, and in one hell of a way they did it. They were part of a team. Without team effort, without them, the fight would have been lost. All of the links in the chain pulled together and the chain became unbreakable.

Don't forget, you men don't know that I'm here. No mention of that fact is to be made in any letters. The world is not supposed to know what the hell happened to me. I'm not supposed to be commanding this army. I'm not even supposed to be here in England. Let the first bastards to find out be the Goddamned Germans. Someday I want to see them raise up on their piss-soaked hind legs and howl, "Jesus Christ, it's the Goddamned US army again and that son-of-a-fucking-bitch Patton." We want to get the hell over there. The quicker we clean up this Goddamned mess, the quicker we can take a little jaunt against the purple pissing Japs and clean out their nest, too. Before the Goddamned marines get all of the credit.

Sure, we want to go home. We want this war over with. The quickest way to get it over with is to go get the bastards who started it. The quicker they are whipped, the quicker we can go home. The shortest way home is through Berlin and Tokyo. And when we get to Berlin, I am personally going to shoot that paper hanging son-of-a-bitch Hitler. Just like I'd shoot a snake!

When a man is lying in a shell hole, if he just stays there all day, a German will get to him eventually. The hell with that idea. The hell with taking it. My men don't dig foxholes. I don't want them to. Foxholes only slow up an offensive. Keep moving. And don't give the enemy time to dig one either. We'll win this war, but we'll win it only by fighting and by showing the Germans that we've got more guts than they have; or ever will have. We're not going to just shoot the sons-of-bitches, we're going to rip out their living Goddamned guts and use them to grease the treads of our tanks. We're going to murder those lousy Hun cock suckers by the bushel-fucking-basket.

War is a bloody, killing business. You've got to spill their blood, or they will spill yours. Rip them up the belly. Shoot them in the guts. When shells are hitting all around you and you wipe the dirt off your face and realise that instead of dirt it's the blood and guts of what once was your best friend beside you, you'll know what to do!

I don't want to get any messages saying, "I am holding my position." We are not holding a Goddamned thing. Let the Germans do that. We are advancing constantly and we are not interested in holding onto anything, except the enemy's balls. We are going to twist his balls and kick the living shit out of him all of the time. Our basic plan of operation is to advance and to keep on advancing regardless of whether we have to go over, under, or through the enemy. We are going to go through him like crap through a goose; like shit through a tin horn!

From time to time there will be some complaints that we are pushing our people too hard. I don't give a good Goddamn about such complaints. I believe in the old and sound rule that an ounce of sweat will save a gallon of blood. The harder WE push, the more Germans we will kill. The more Germans we kill, the fewer of our men will be killed. Pushing means fewer casualties. I want you all to remember that.

There is one great thing that you men will all be able to say after this war is over and you are home once again. You may be thankful that twenty years from now when you are sitting by the fireplace with your grandson on your knee and he asks you what you did in the great World War II, you WON'T have to cough, shift him to the other knee and say, "Well, your Granddaddy shovelled shit in Louisiana." No, Sir, you can look him straight in the eye and say, "Son, your Granddaddy

> *rode with the Great US army and a Son-of-a-Goddamned-Bitch named Georgie Patton!"*
>
> *And remember, all of you, you never saw me or heard me today. None of you. I'm a ghost.*
>
> *That is all.'* [18]

The General's speech worked small miracles. The American GIs were buoyant, surfing on a wave of gung-ho optimism. Back in Lyme Regis, the troops didn't know it, but it was just one day before they were due to leave for their embarkation points. A final treat for the US troops was organised. And it was a major event. The James Cagney review show was to take place at a red-bricked hall, which in peacetime had been the boys' club in Church Street. James Cagney was coming to Lyme together with a variety show called, 'Keep 'em Rolling'. Whilst Cagney was best-known for his gangster and street fighter roles, he'd actually grown up in vaudeville. In 1942 he'd starred as the vaudeville-trooper, George M. Cohan, in the film, 'Yankee Doodle Dandy', in which he danced and sang, winning the Oscar for 'best actor'. The show in Lyme was to feature many of his routines from that hit film.

The Lavenders' black troops invited their local girls along, and Jo arrived with Franklin, together with

Eugene and Edith. Ruth hadn't dated the US boys. She was still too much the product of her upbringing to get closely involved with the soldiers, or, as yet, any other young men. Although Jo asked Franklin, he was unable to get Ruth a ticket, and she was left, sadly dejected back at 'Lavenders'. The queue to get in was something of an ordeal, but a well-tempered and very noisy one. Inside, it was a sardine-tin-like crush of bodies. The GIs were raucous and appreciative. The show was tremendous. An exhilarating, all-American helter-skelter ride of loud, brash music, comedy and dance. Cagney had opened the show saying: *"I'm here to dance a few jigs, sing a few songs, say hello to the boys, and that's all."*

The foursome left the makeshift theatre on a high, and as they approached Cobb Gate, the men offered round Lucky Strikes and lit up cigarettes for the girls and themselves. A gaggle of nine or ten white GIs spotted the group outside off the Vaults public house, just near the sea wall.
"What you got there, boy, you knows your kind aren't allowed PX lighters." Before Eugene and Franklin could even reply, three of the GIs had grabbed the black GIs, pinning their arms back. Then in flash it happened. Afterwards, Jo wasn't certain what she'd seen. But one of the white GIs had pulled out a bayonet and was thrusting it repeatedly into Franklin's chest.

Another white GI was screaming for blood, waving his knife around above his head. He lunged with it indiscriminately. Who he killed or injured didn't seem to matter. There was screaming all around. Jo's wailing was lost in the madness and mayhem. More and more GIs were fighting. Whites against blacks, with some locals wading in, seemingly almost entirely on the side of the coloured GIs.

A police whistle sounded. It was the local English police sergeant, but no-one was taking notice. Maybe 200 men and women were involved. It was a scene of total anarchy and increasing carnage. The police sergeant yelled for order, then he took out a sheet of paper and after more blows on his whistle, shouted out a section from the 'Riot Act'. It didn't make any difference. The fighting continued, bloody and intense, fuelled by pent up emotions, testosterone and alcohol. It seemed an age, but after about 15 minutes two jeeps with American Military Police arrived. There were more whistles of a different tone and some shots were fired. The crowd quietened as the MPs appeared to randomly hit a few soldiers with their batons. The MPs were all white soldiers and appeared to target the coloured GIs.

And then it was over. In the aftermath, two black GIs lay on the ground, dead – both Eugene and Jo's boyfriend, Franklin. There were another 16 injured GIs, plus about half a dozen Lyme residents, including Jack the Gas, who had tried to intervene on behalf of the black GIs. Being wartime, it didn't get reported in the press. It was treated as a US military matter, hushed up and dealt with under US laws, even though the incident had occurred in Lyme Regis in Dorset. Jo and Edith mourned their loved ones but could obtain no news on their murderers.

The day after the incident, or 'riot' as the locals in Lyme called it, the American troops were gone. Along with their Canadian and British allies, they gathered in assembly areas along the coast of southern England, waiting for the signal to embark for D-Day. Some of the GIs involved in the Lyme mayhem were most probably held at Shepton Mallet prison,[19] and perhaps tried and convicted under US military laws. Maybe they were hung, or just maybe, they became even more infamous, featuring in another writer's tale that became known, world-wide as 'The Dirty Dozen'.

Endnotes

US officers outside a hotel in Lyme Regis

This is fiction. Most of the main characters are total inventions. However, the circumstances of the American GIs training in and around Lyme Regis, Dorset and Devon, and their preparations for the Overlord invasion on D-Day in June 1944 are based on research, together with written accounts and interviews conducted by the author. But, some aspects of the chronology and the exact details of events are speculative 'fictions'. Likewise, the author has taken fictional liberties with the location of a number of events recorded in the narrative and conflated some together. For historians, even in the fact-based accounts of this period there is some disagreement about details, such as exactly when the 1st Division were on exercises at Slapton Sands. Eisenhower and Patton did make their speeches – probably over and over again in different locations, with minor changes. The versions here are based on historical versions available on the internet.

The real-life person I partly based the character of Ricky upon, had by the summer of 1944, managed to squirrel away over £400. In fact, enough to buy an old cottage at the point when he left school to go to agricultural college. Similarly, the character that Jack the Gas is partly reminiscent of, told the author:
"I'll never forget the day they left for the invasion. The stuff they left behind. They said to me, 'Get that bloody van up here, pronto'. Dear, oh dear, you'd never

believe it. I had a van-load."

We do know that the 1st Infantry Division embarked from Portland and Weymouth on 5th June, to land to the north of Colleville sur mer, Normandie early on the morning of 6th June. The 1st Infantry Division comprised more than 34,000 American troops and over 3,000 vehicles, which were assigned to the most heavily defended and fortified of all the beachheads, codenamed Omaha. A compacted version of the events at Omaha beach featured in the opening sequences of the film, 'Saving Private Ryan'.

E.M. Nathanson, the author of *'The Dirty Dozen'*, introduced his book, saying:

"This story is fiction. I have heard a legend that there might have been men like them, but nowhere in the archives of the United States Government, or in its military history did I find it recorded."

The 'friendly invasion' really did take place. And, it left an indelible mark on many lives, British and American alike. The famous writer and historian, A.J.P. Herbert, wrote a tribute to the American troops' time in Britain, to celebrate the opening of a London club at 201 Piccadilly for the 'Allied navies, armies and air forces':

'Goodbye GI. Don't leave us quite alone,
Somewhere in England we must write in stone,
"How Britain was Invaded by the Yanks"
And under that a big hearty "Thanks".'

As for the end of segregation in the American armed forces (and in many of the American states), that took a long time to achieve. According to Philip McGuire, a black history professor, in 'Taps for a Jim Crow Army', he cogently argues that it took the Vietnam War, coupled with the rise of Civil Rights Movement to accomplish. Even then, there remain even today vestiges of racism and discrimination. You could argue that President Obama is still fighting against it. McGuire suggests that:
"By the 1980s, integration of the armed forces was an accomplished fact...But the most glaring recognition of an integrated armed forces was President George Bush's 1989 appointment of General Colin L. Powell as the first African-American chairman of the Joint Chiefs of Staff."

* * * * * * * * * * *

The author gives especial thanks to Jo Draper, and in the past, John Fowles, who was very supportive of the project – they have both served Lyme Regis Museum well; the D-Day Museum at Southsea; Bridport

Library; The Sunday reception staff at Teignmouth Museum; Nigel Clarke and Craig Sullivan for help at the research stage; Christine Harding for putting up with me during my early research, and most of all to the very supportive people who shared their remembrances of wartime in Dorset and Devon, and in particular their memories of the American friendly invasion. Like many pieces of creative writing, perhaps especially 'fact-ions', this story has actually taken many years to complete. It started out as an idea discussed in a general way in correspondence firstly with John Fowles with whom I swapped information and memorabilia. This was followed, more than a decade later by lengthy field research in and around Lyme interviewing locals and some American ex-GIs. Add to this, the accumulation and reading of three shelf-fulls of books, publications and internet resources, and eventually the actual writing.

With my thanks and best wishes

John Fowles

Thanks are also due to Alan's friends and colleagues for their helpful and constructive comments on the 'story' as it unfolded. They are: Phil Bayliss; Margaret Greenfields; Ric Rogers; Andy Wood; Oliver Carfrae and Deirdre Howard-Williams.

Notes

1. Operation Sealion. Information about Hitler's invasion plans were intercepted at Bletchley Park using the 'Enigma' machine-code breaking apparatus as early as July 17th 1940. The invasion plan was codenamed Seelöwe (Sealion in English), the plan was also sometimes referred to as 'Operation Smith'. Hitler's original, ambitious plan, was to mount a naval attack on the southern English coast from Kent right through to the Dorset border with Devon at Lyme Regis and beyond to Seaton.

2. Mrs May's six points were widely reported and commented upon in the British press. The first report was published in the 'Sunday Pictorial' on September 6th 1943, following a women's meeting called by Mrs May, who was the vicar's wife in the village of Worple, outside of Weston-super-Mare.

3. The locations of the US HQs are based on those cited in Robin Pearce's book, 'Seven months to D-Day'.

4. The marching chants or cadences were known as 'Jodies' after a character often recurring in the chants themselves. An army v-disk ('V for victory') issued in 1944 suggests that the earliest chant was instigated by a *"Negro soldier by the name of Willie Duckworth,*

on detached service with the Provisional Training Center, who was chanting to build up the spirits of his comrades. It was not long before the infectious rhythm was spreading throughout the ranks. Footweary soldiers started to pick up their step in cadence with the growing chorus of hearty male voices. Instead of a down trodden, fatigued company, here marched 200 soldiers with heads up, a spring to their step, and happy smiles on their faces. This transformation occurred with the beginning of the Duckworth Chant."

5. From 1940 onwards President Roosevelt had imposed a target of ten per cent of blacks in the army in each theatre of operation and he insisted that the same apply to the US army in Britain. Churchill's Foreign Secretary, Anthony Eden, had told the American Ambassador Winnant that *"the British climate is badly suited to negroes"*. But the black troops arrived and question of whether to adopt the American 'colour bar' and segregation in Britain was raised in the House of Commons, where Churchill said that he hoped that *"without any action on my part the points of view of all concerned will be mutually understood and respected"*. The reality was that a set of double-standards was adopted, with the War Office covertly supporting the US army segregation policy, without publicly acknowledging the fact. During the Cabinet discussion on the issue, Lord Cranborne, the Colonial Secretary,

reported that one of his own black officials had been barred from a regular restaurant for fear of offending US officers. Churchill is reported to have replied, "...*if he takes a banjo with him they'll think he's one of the band*".

6. The War Office officially avoided issuing anything in writing about agreeing with a colour bar, however, General Arthur Dowler, the senior administrative officer in Southern Command issued 'Notes on Relations with Coloured Troops' to District Commanders. In it, he spoke of a "*generality*" of blacks having "*a simple mental outlook*". Because of the existence of the 'Notes', the Secretary of State for War, Sir James Grigg wanted to issue an official set of advice to British officers for them to be able to "*interpret the facts and history of the colour question*". In the event, Churchill's Cabinet approved a revised set of Dowler's 'Notes' for issue to officers after they had been seen by Eisenhower.

7. Stalag Luft VI. The camp located in East Prussia, now Lithuania, was opened in about June 1943 to admit British and Canadian NCOs, including those who were former prisoners at Stalag Luft I, Barth, and Dulag Luft. Their senior officer was Dixie Deans. Later on in 1944, Americans were also interred there. However, the camp actually had a far longer history, and under

the name Stalag 1C it had been used for Polish and then French and Belgian POWs from 1940.

8. John Costello in his book 'Love, Sex and War' says, *"...the prodigious sexual activity of GIs in Britain was revealed by the VD statistics, which rose from twenty cases per thousand to almost sixty per thousand amongst the American forces stationed here"*. The Ministry of Health was correctly alarmed and launched its 'Let Knowledge Grow' campaign. The campaign worked and there was a decline in the VD statistics during the later part of 1943 and into 1944, though there was an increase again as a result of 'last fling' romances just before D-Day. A wonderful anecdote concerned an English prostitute who had infected at least five US airmen at the Shipham airbase in Norfolk. She actually wrote to the Ministry of Health asking that they should post a note at the airbase saying that she had been successfully treated. Her request was declined!

9. Jim Crow laws and customs of segregation and discrimination were still widely accepted in America, especially in the Southern States at the time of World War II. US Brigadier General Benjamin O. Davies wrote a memorandum to General Peterson on 9th November 1943 stating that:
"The coloured man in uniform is expected by the War Department to develop high morale in a community

that offers him nothing except humiliation and mistreatment. Military training does not develop a spirit of cheerful acceptance of Jim-Crow laws and customs...On the training fields the development of morale does not take into consideration Jim-Crow laws and customs...Officers of the War Department General Staff have refused to attempt any remedial action to eliminate Jim-Crow."

10. 'The People's War' was a term used to cover all activities on the Home Front in Britain during the Second World War. A key feature was the War Savings Campaign. This was run by Sir Robert Kindersley on behalf of the British Government, mainly as an extension of the National Savings Movement which he had led before the war.

11. Savings groups were organised in each local community throughout the country. The War Savings Campaign encouraged thrift at an individual level and brought together the community by fund-raising for large-scale campaigns such as the 'Spitfire Fund' (1940), 'War Weapons Week' (1941), 'Warship Weeks' (1941/1942), 'Wings For Victory Week' (1943) and 'Salute the Soldier Week' (1944).

12. Between January and May 1944, a succession of amphibious training operations were planned by

the Americans in conjunction with the allied forces. Operation Duck took place first, then Fox, Muskrat, Beaver and Trousers before the disastrous Exercise Tiger in April, and finally Exercise Fabius in May. In the book 'The Land we left behind' by Rose-Price and Parnell, suggests that 200 lives were lost to friendly fire during the practice exercises.

13. 'Going over the hill' was a colloquial phrase to mean going 'absent without leave', or absconding.

14. Joe Louis Barrow, known around the world as the 'Brown Bomber' was arguably one of the greatest boxers in history and a positive role-model for African-Americans. His period as World Heavyweight Champion stretched from 1937 to 1949, during which he fought 26 title fights. However, as an American sports ambassador, Louis travelled more than 21,000 miles and staged 96 boxing exhibitions before two million soldiers. His exhibition and military charity bouts raised about 90 thousand dollars for the US war effort, and even more in terms of positive publicity and morale raising.

15. An amusing observation on the sexual revolution in England during the 'American' years was made by Quentin Crisp, who declared, *"Never in the history of sex was so much offered to so many by so few."*

16. According to Viv Wilson in her book 'Teignmouth at War 1939-45', the exact numbers for Teignmouth were: 22 air attacks; 228 houses destroyed; 2,250 damaged; 79 people killed and 151 casualties.

17. These diary extracts are exactly as given on the website: www.generalpatton.org

18. The Patton speech is as close to the original as is possible, but in reality it was most likely to have been addressed to his own American Third Army just before D-Day. The 'version' included here is from the research of Charles M. Province, available at: www.pattonhq.com/speech.html

19. Shepton Mallet prison in Somerset became a US military establishment in the middle of 1942 and remained a wholly American-run establishment until September 1945. By the end of 1944 it held 768 military prisoners. During its time under US governance, under the aegis of the United States of America (Military Forces) Act 1942, 18 inmates were executed; 16 by hanging and two by firing squad.

Alan Dearling: www.enablerpublications.co.uk

World War II and the American GIs: sources

Live ammunition was used in the exercises at Slapton Sands

Adams, Neil. *Lyme Regis 1939-45: A boy's memories.* Philpot Museum, Lyme Regis, 1984.

After the Battle magazine, published quarterly by Battle of Prints International (esp. issues 44: The other D-Days and 103: Spielberg's D-Day).

Albert, Jonah. *Information from Channel 4 on Brown Babies programme and background.*

Allen, Thomas B.. 'Untold Stories of D-Day' in *National Geographic* magazine, June 2002.

Archer, Fred. *When Village Bells Were Silent.* Hodder and Stoughton, 1975.

Austin, Barbara. *Lyme Regis's mayor's personal recollections of WWII.*

Baker, Janet. *The children they left behind.* Volume 4, Number 2, April, 1996 edition of 'Lest We Forget'.

Bass, Richard. *Regiments in Lyme Regis in WW II.* Philpot Museum, Lyme Regis, 1988.

Belsey, James and Reid, Helen. *West at War.* Redcliffe Press, 1990.

Bennett, Pat. *Signed deposition regarding childhood in Lyme.*

Bingley, Xandra. *Bertie, May and Mrs Fish: Country Memories of Wartime.* Harper Perennial, 2005.

Binns, Stewart, Carter, Lucy and Wood, Adrian. *Britain at War in Colour.* Carlton Books, 2000.

Bradbeer, Grace. *The Land Changed its Face: The evacuation of South Hams 1943-44.* Devon Books, 2nd edition, 1997.

Braithwaite, Brian *et al.. The Home Front: the best of Good Housekeeping 1939-1945*. Leopard Books, 1995.

Bridgehead Sentinel museum news from the Big Red One, First Division Cantigny Museum.

Bridport News, The. *January 1943-end of June 1944 editions.* Viewed on microfiche, Bridport Library.

Briggs, Susan. *Keep smiling through: The Home Front 1939-45*. Book Club Associates, 1975.

Broad, Richard. *Dunkeswell: Parish and People.* Richard Broad, 1994.

Brooks, Stephen and Eckstein, Eve. *Operation Overlord: The History of D-Day and the Overlord Embroidery.* Ashford, 1989.

Cawthorne, Nigel. *Fighting them on the beaches.* Arcturus Publishing, 2002.

Chard and Illminster News. *The War Years 1939-45.* Chard History Group, 1996.

Clarke, Roger. *Personal recollections of being evacuated to Lyme Regis area.*

Collier, Richard. *D-Day: 06/06/1944.* Cassell, 1992.

Costello, John. *Love, sex and war 1939-1945.* Pan Books, 1986.

Croad, Mary. *Interview on recollections of Lyme Regis in WW II.*

Daily Telegraph. *50th Anniversary of the Normandy Landings special issue.* June 3rd, 1994.

D-Day Museum, Portsmouth, personal

communications from Andrew Whitmarsh, Military History Officer.
D-Day Study Weekend, Bridport April 2004. *Personal Notes from the two day seminar.*
Disney, Francis. *Shepton Mallet Prison.* Whitstone Press, 1992.
Drez, Ronald J.. *Voices of D-Day.* Louisiana State University Press, 1994.
Earle, Peter. *Monmouth's Rebels.* Weidenfeld and Nicholson, 1977.
Farrington, Karen. *Witness to World War II.* Abbeydale Press, 1995.
Forty, George. *Frontline Dorset: A county at war 1939-45.* Dorset Books, 1994.
Foster, Andy and Furst, Steve. *Radio Comedy 1938-1968.* Virgin Publishing, 1996.
Fox, Richard. *Local Lyme Regis historian's recollections.*
Garrett, Margaret. *Personal memories of Lyme in wartime.*
Gerryts, Rene. 'Sir James salutes all the American heroes' in *Bridport and Lyme Regis News,* September 27, 2002.
Gosling, Ted and Chapple, Roy. *East Devon at War.* Allan Sutton Publishing, 1995.
Hall, Anne. *Land Girl.* Ex Libris Press, 1993.
Hall, Doreen. *Bridport during the Second World War.* Personal communication.

Harclerode, Peter. *'Go to it!' The illustrated history of the 6th Airborne Division.* Caxton Editions, 2000.
Hardy, Donald. *Personal memories of Lyme in wartime.*
Hawkins, Mac. *Somerset at War, 1939-1945.* Hawk Editions, 1996.
Healey, Tim. *Life on the Home Front.* Reader's Digest Association, 1994 edition.
Hennessy, Peter. *Never again.* Vintage, 1992.
Herald Express publications. *D for Destiny.* Special 32 page West Country tribute newspaper, June 1st 2004.
Hersey, Lucinda and Mason, Catherine. *The West Country at War.* Broadcast Books, 1995.
HMSO. *Union Jack: a scrapbook of British Forces' Newspapers 1939-45.* HMSO, 1989.
Holt, Major and Mrs. *Normandy Landing Beaches: Battlefield Guide.* Leo Cooper, 1999.
Hopkinson, Tom. *Picture Post 1938-50.* Penguin Books, 1970.
Hoyt, Edwin. *The Invasion before Normandy.* Robert Hale, 1985.
Huggett, Frank. *Goodnight Sweetheart: Songs and Memories of the Second World War.* W.H.Allen, 1979.
Inglis, Ruth. *The Children's War: Evacuation 1939-1945.* William Collins and Sons, 1989.
Irving, David. *Churchill's War, vol. 2: Triumph in Adversity.* Focal Point, 2001.
Keegan, John. *The World at War 1939-1945.* The

Illustrated London News, Bracken Books, 1990.
Koenig, William J.. *Americans at War*. Bison Books, 1980.
Lanfear, Harold. *Extract from the Draft Memoirs of Harold Lanfear: Yanks at Lyme Regis*. Philpot Museum, Lyme Regis.
Legg, Rodney. *Dorset's War 1939-45*. Wincanton Press, 1986.
Legg, Rodney. *Wartime Dorset: The Complete History*. Dorset Publishing at Wincanton Press, 2000.
Lund, H. *Personal recollections of the 1939-45 war in Lyme Regis*. Philpot Museum, Lyme Regis, 1979.
Luxton, Fred, local Home Guard in WW II. *Deposition and interview*.
Lynn, Vera. *We'll meet again: A personal and social history of World War Two*. Sidgwick and Jackson, 1989.
MacGregor, J. Morris, jnr.. *Integration of the Armed Forces*. Center of Military History, Washington DC, 1985.
Matanle, Ivor. *World War II*. Colour Library Books, 1989.
Mayer, S.L.. *Hitler's Wartime Picture Magazine: Signal*. Bison Publishing, 1976.
McGuire, Philip. *Taps for a Jim Crow army: Letters from Black soldiers in World War II*. University Press of Kentucky, 1993 edition.
Murphy, John. *Dorset at War!* Dorset Publishing Company, 1979.

Nathanson, E.M.. *The Dirty Dozen.* Cassell Military Paperbacks, 1966.

Nicholson, Mavis. *What did you do in the War, Mummy? Women in World War II.* Chatto and Windus, 1995.

O'Neill, Gilda. *Our Street.* Penguin Books, 2003.

Odham's. *The fifth year of the war in pictures.* Odham's Press, 1945.

Parrish, Thomas. *The Simon and Schuster Encyclopedia of World War II.* Simon and Schuster, New York, 1978.

Parry, Dan. *D-Day 6.6.44: The World's Greatest Invasion.* BBC Books with the Imperial War Museum, 2004.

Patrick, Neil, ed.. *All our working lives.* Yours magazine, undated.

Patrick, Neil, ed.. *Life in Uniform.* Yours magazine, undated.

Pearce, Robin. *Seven months to D-Day: an American Regiment in Dorset.* Dovecote Press, 2000.

Peck, Edward. *Letter from GI in 99th Infantry Division.*

Perkins, Charles. *Children of the Storm: childhood memories of World War II.* Wordwright Publishing, USA, 1998.

Philpot Museum, Lyme Regis. *Various holdings including passes for the Cobb Harbour and oral history interviews by John Fowles and notes from Jo*

Draper, custodian/curator.
Picture Post magazine – various 1944 editions.
Hulton's National Weekly.
Piekalkiewicz, Janusz. *The Air War 1939-1945.* Blandford Press, 1985.
Pimlott, John, ed.. *Images of War: eyewitness accounts of World War II, in four volumes.* Marshall Cavendish/ Imperial War Museum, 1988.
Pitt, Barrie. *50th Anniversary of D-Day.* Harrington Kilbride/Imperial War Museum, 1994.
Potter, Lou, Miles, William and Rosenblum, Nina. *The Liberators: fighting on two fronts in World War II.* Harcourt Brace Jovanovich, Orlando, 1992.
Reprinted by the University Press of Kentucky, 1993.
Reynolds, David. *Rich Relations: The American occupation of Britain 1942-1945.* Harper-Collins, 1996.
Rose, E.J.. *The Axminster to Lyme Regis Railway.* Kingfisher Railway Productions, 1982.
Rose-Price, Robin and Parnell, Jean. *The Land we left behind.* Orchard Publications, 2004.
Shilleto, Carl and Tolhurst, Mike. *D-Day and the Battle for Normandy.* Windrush Press, 2000.
Shute, Neville. *The Chequer Board.* Pan, 1947.
Small, Ken. *The Forgotten Dead.* Bloomsbury, 1993 edition.
Smith, Graham. *When Jim Crow met John Bull: Black American soldiers in World War II Britain.* I.B.Taurus

& Co, 1987.
Stafford, David. *Ten Days to D-Day.* Abacus, 2004.
Stevens, Derek. *Interviews by phone and in person on Lyme Regis during WW II.*
Strange, Joan. *Despatches from the Home Front: the War Diaries of Joan Strange 1939-45.* Monarch Publications, 1989.
Teeman, Tim. 'Still Daisy after all these years' in *The Times,* May 4th, 2002.
Thomas, Leslie. *The Magic Army.* Eyre Methuen, 1981.
Trump, H.J.. *Teignmouth.* Phillimore and Co, 2005.
Turner, Symphony. *Personal memories of her mother in wartime Lyme Regis.*
Vaughan-Thomas, Wynford. *D-Day to Victory 1944-45.* Collins, 1984.
Virden, Jenel. *Good-bye Piccadilly: British war brides in America.* University of Illinois, 1996.
Waller, Joan and Vaughan-Rees, Michael. *Women in Uniform 1939-43.* Papermac, 1989.
War and Navy Departments (US, Washington). *A Short Guide to Great Britain.* 1942.
Wasley, Gerald. *Devon at War 1939-45.* Devon Books, 1994.
Web sites including: 1st Infantry Division; BigRedOne; NARA; PBS; VOA News; Channel 4 Black History season; Blackpresence; Imperial War Museum; D-Day museum and BBC – People's War

and the inevitable Wikipedia.
Webb, Edwin and Duncan, John. *Blitz over Britain.* Spellmount Ltd, 1990.
Whiting, Charles. *'44: in combat on the Western Front from Normandy to the Ardennes.* Century Publishing, 1984.
Wicks, Ben. *No time to wave goodbye: True stories of Britain's 3,500,000 evacuees.* Bloomsbury, 1988.
Williams, Mavis. *Lumber Jill.* Ex Libris Press, 1994.
Wilson, Viv. *Teignmouth at War, 1939-45.* Viv Wilson, 2000.
Wilson, Viv. *Teginmouth at War 2.* Viv Wilson, 2002.
Wilson, Viv. *Teignmouth and its people 1935 to 1953.* Viv Wilson, 2005.
Wiscombe, Jack. *Personal memories of Lyme in wartime.*
Wright, Michael. *World at War.* Readers Digest Association, 1989.
Yass, Marion. *The Home Front.* Wayland Publishers, 1971.

GIs and LSTs practise landings at Slapton Sands

Alan Dearling

For all of his life Alan has written articles, books and helped other people publish their works. Along that journey he has been a youth worker, social worker, senior university research fellow and a publisher with the Scottish Office, Longman, Pitman, Joseph Rowntree Foundation, the Chartered Institute of Housing and Russell House Publishing. He is currently a director on the boards of the Authors' Licensing and Collecting Society and the Copyright Licensing Agency.

To date he has authored about forty books, which have sold in the order of 250,000 copies. Most have been non-fiction covering a wide range of subjects from creative work with young people; work with young offenders; festivals, new Travellers and alternative lifestyles; music; housing and social policy; Africa; Australia and Scotland. His earlier novel, 'The Sigil', was described by 'Cathy Come Home' author, Jeremy Sandford:

"I read it with great pleasure. I like it very much for its gentleness. It's charming, delightful, tender even. I got involved with Jenn and thought her a lovely character/ creation. And I thought the ending, which has many reverberations, is excellent."

Alan currently lives in Eyemouth in the Scottish borders and enjoys a pint or three of traditional, alcoholic apple juice. Contact Alan through his website: www.enablerpublications.co.uk